**Quin Farrell was a real, live hero.**

With just enough light from the moon to watch him sleep, Luz became fascinated. Despite the beard stubble, he was a good-looking man. His features were rugged, masculine. Her gaze went to his cheek and she wondered how he'd gotten that nasty scar.

Protecting his country?

Unable to help herself, she reached out and ran a finger down its length, and a thrill shot through her all the way to her toes.

Before she could define the feeling, Quin's eyes shot open and his hand manacled her wrist. Her breath caught in her throat. She couldn't say a word, couldn't look away, couldn't move her hand.

"What are you doing?"

As she slid in next to him, a sense of anticipation that had been building since she'd met him intensified. "Trying to get closer. You make me feel safe."

Groaning softly, Quin covered her mouth with his. Luz's heart began to thud. Even knowing she was about to lose her virginity, she parted her lips and let him have his way with her mouth.

Curse his McKenna blood and the legacy that went with it!

# PATRICIA ROSEMOOR

# RESCUING THE VIRGIN

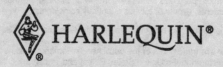

## HARLEQUIN®

TORONTO • NEW YORK • LONDON
AMSTERDAM • PARIS • SYDNEY • HAMBURG
STOCKHOLM • ATHENS • TOKYO • MILAN • MADRID
PRAGUE • WARSAW • BUDAPEST • AUCKLAND

Thanks to my editor Denise Zaza
for letting me push the envelope a little farther.

Recycling programs
for this product may
not exist in your area.

ISBN-13: 978-0-373-69395-5
ISBN-10:    0-373-69395-8

RESCUING THE VIRGIN

www.eHarlequin.com

**Printed in U.S.A.**

## ABOUT THE AUTHOR

Patricia Rosemoor has always had a fascination with dangerous love. She loves bringing a mix of thrills and chills and romance to Harlequin Intrigue readers. She's won a Golden Heart from Romance Writers of America and Reviewers' Choice and Career Achievement Awards from *Romantic Times BOOKreviews*. She teaches Writing Popular Fiction and Suspense-Thriller Writing in the Fiction Writing Department of Columbia College Chicago. Check out her Web site, www.PatriciaRosemoor.com. You can contact Patricia either via e-mail at Patricia@PatriciaRosemoor.com, or through the publisher at Patricia Rosemoor, c/o Harlequin/Silhouette Books, 233 Broadway, New York, NY 10279.

## Books by Patricia Rosemoor

Don't miss any of our special offers. Write to us at the following address for information on our newest releases.

Harlequin Reader Service
U.S.: 3010 Walden Ave., P.O. Box 1325, Buffalo, NY 14269
Canadian: P.O. Box 609, Fort Erie, Ont. L2A 5X3

# CAST OF CHARACTERS

*Quinlan (Quin) McKenna Farrell*—The ICE agent will do anything to shut down the human trafficking operation.

*Luz (Lucille) Delgado*—She won't stop until she finds her half-brother.

*Diego Ortiz*—Why did Luz's half-brother go missing in the first place?

*El Jefe*—How does the elusive leader of the human trafficking operation keep his identity secret?

*Cesar Galindo*—Did the leader of the vigilante group have other loyalties?

*John Ward*—What was the owner of Hunt Ranch really up to?

*Bianca Ramos*—Is the former victim now working for *El Jefe*?

*Bobby Ray Martin*—Did the foreman of the ranch have another job on the side?

*Aaron Keller*—How much would Quin's partner put on the line for him?

# Prologue

He could hear them behind him.

He heard them beyond the wheeze of his own gasping breath, through the rush of blood filling his head, above the slap-slap of his bare feet against the rocky earth. He heard the horses' hooves and the wail of the dogs and the excited voices of the two gringos hunting the most exotic animal of all.

*Him...*

They'd given him a head start. Not much, but something. They'd told him to run as fast as he could to reach the river before they caught up with him. The *Rio Bravo del Norte* would offer him a safe haven...if he didn't drown first. Barely knowing how to swim, he prayed it would be a low spot, that he could simply walk across. Then he would be free and could get back to his own.

As he rocketed toward freedom, he thought about his family. His friends. Everyone left behind.

Were they waiting for him or did they already think he was dead?

He could sense the river ahead, could smell the water, could hear its rush. He just couldn't see it.

The sounds behind him were now getting louder. The hunters were narrowing the gap. He ran faster, harder. Blind with fear, he almost ran straight off the canyon cliff...

Just in time, he stopped himself, a shower of small rocks spraying down into the foaming river below. He crossed himself and said a quick prayer.

Rapids!

Panic spread through him, added a fine sheen to his burnished copper skin. His stomach threatened him, but with what? It was empty, had been for days.

He couldn't cross into Mexico here—he would drown for sure!

Even as he turned to look for a way out, one of the dogs hit him mid-chest and he stumbled backward. A whistle called off the creature before it could go for his throat, but his feet were already dancing on the uneven edge of the canyon cliff.

The leader said something in English he couldn't understand. The two men laughed and the second man raised his high-powered rifle fitted with a scope.

The first shot blew him back. The earth gave way and the watery grave rushed up to meet him.

# *Chapter One*

"C'mon, c'mon!"

Luz Delgado slapped the steering wheel of her SUV as though that would help get her across the international bridge that spanned the Rio Grande into Nuevo Laredo, Mexico, faster. The traffic was what it was, barely inching forward. Stop and go. Stop and go. She could see construction equipment ahead. She should have walked the bridge across the river as were the dozens of people on foot. Not needing to be further stressed, she tried to tune out the slow-down.

Making a call on her cell, she got nothing but an instruction to leave a message. "Where are you, Diego? Why haven't you returned my calls?"

She hadn't heard from her half brother for three days now. His girlfriend, Pilar Morales, had disappeared, and Diego had been determined to find her. Luz had made him promise to call her every day so she would know he was all right. He *had* called…a few times. Then the calls had stopped coming, making Luz wonder if Diego had met the same fate as his girlfriend, whatever that might be.

Not knowing what had happened to him was killing her. She'd had to find out and so she had abandoned the safety of the bookstore where she worked, where she'd hidden from life for nearly five years. For the last half decade, she'd preferred reading about life rather than experiencing it. But Diego's disappearance had pushed her to act quite out of character.

She'd left San Antonio for a quick trip into Mexico, in hopes that she would be able to see for herself that her brother was all right. She was all he had, really. Cancer had taken his mother from him when he was a teenager. He must have relatives somewhere in Mexico, but his mother had left her family and had never spoken of them.

The tangle of traffic just ahead finally seemed to straighten itself out as it rounded the road repairs. Luz found herself moving along at last, then quickly made it through the customs and immigration checkpoint.

Now in Mexico, Luz entered another world, one of open-air mercados and street vendors, of mariachis and landscaped plazas alive with families, children shrieking as they played around the fountains. Beggars with signs saying they were hungry and hucksters hawking cheap wares swarmed around every vehicle on the street. She'd been here before to visit Diego, but she never felt quite comfortable.

Luz drove past the mayhem—much of it, like the horse-drawn buggies, calculated to attract the tourist dollar—to a quieter part of the border town.

She passed mostly one-and two-story buildings until she reached her brother's block, distinctive because of the clay-colored arcade building, whose arches gave entry to the shaded walkway and shop doors. Also distinctive were the three floors of apartments above the shops. Diego lived on the top floor over a farmacia, a supermercado and a small handicraft shop.

Parking was nearly impossible, but today she was lucky and found a spot directly across the street.

Getting out of the SUV, Luz felt unsettled, almost as if she were being watched. The weird feeling sending a chill down her spine and making her stomach knot had to be from worry over Diego. She looked around and assured herself no one was paying her any mind.

Well, almost no one.

A couple of teenagers stopped in the street to stare at her and whistle. "Hey, *belleza, ven conmigo!*"

Even though she perfectly understood the kid's come on, Luz ignored him. She was used to being hit on, whether in English or Spanish. Still, the thought of confronting the kid bothered her, made her pulse rush a little faster, so she grabbed her bag, beeped her vehicle locked and crossed to the apartment building's courtyard entry.

After pressing her brother's doorbell several times with no response, Luz headed directly for Nuevo Laredo Artesania, owned and run by Jacinta Herrera, Diego's landlady. Fired clay pots spilled into the walkway and hand-carved wood pieces hung from hooks around the doorway. Entering, Luz looked around and oriented herself.

The interior of the store was fitted with old wood and glass displays filled to the brim with silver bracelets and earrings and small and large leather goods. An old *trastero* with doors open featured wearable art—embroidered *camisas* and long skirts and shawls. Luz had been in here only a few times before, but she had always been impressed with the quality of the merchandise.

The thing that impressed her the most, however, was a series of masks lining the wall behind the counter. They were life-size ceramic masks of women's faces. Luz knew they were the missing, suspected victims of human trafficking. The number had increased since she'd last been here.

Shuddering at the thought of people being lifted off the street in the newest incarnation of slavery, Luz looked for the owner.

Jacinta Herrera, a regal sixty-something, silver wings in her long, dark hair framing a gently lined face, was with a customer, a well-heeled younger woman with striking Aztec features and flawless taste. Dressed in a designer, clay-colored suit that played up her exotic heritage, a gem-encrusted snake bracelet decorating one wrist, the customer was paying for a hand-tooled turquoise and coral leather purse. The transaction completed, she left the shop without ever turning her black eyes to Luz. Her disinterest was palpable.

Luz couldn't help but watch her go cross the arcade and approach a black car where a man opened the door for her. A driver?

She was pulled back to her quest when the owner asked in Spanish, "Can I help you?"

Answering in kind, Luz said, "*Señora* Herrera, perhaps you remember me—"

The wrinkled face smoothed as the woman brightened. "Of course. You're Diego Ortiz's sister. Luz, yes? Please, call me Jacinta."

Thankful the woman was welcoming, Luz nodded. "I'm here to see Diego, but he doesn't seem to be home. He hasn't been answering his phone. I'm…worried."

No doubt remembering Luz was a Texan, Jacinta switched to English. "Perhaps he went away for a few days with his woman."

"Several days ago, Pilar…well, she disappeared. Diego said she was taken and he was going to find her. He promised to call, but…" Luz swallowed her spiraling emotion—she had to keep a level head.

"When did you last hear from him?"

"Three days ago. I've called and called."

"Three days…he could be anywhere."

Jacinta Herrera appeared as concerned as she, Luz thought,

trying not to panic as the woman crossed to the face masks and stared at them for a moment.

Luz shook her head. "You don't think—"

"I think anything might have happened. The drug cartel in this area is very dangerous."

"Diego didn't do drugs. And he wouldn't have sold them, either. He hates what drugs have done to people he knows."

"What about his woman?"

"Pilar? I-I don't know. He never said anything about it if she was into drugs. If she was…do you really think dealing with the drug trade had something to do with her disappearance?"

Jacinta shrugged. "Terrible things happen to people in this part of the world." She looked again to the masks. Touched one. "My own niece and her teenage daughter…"

Luz gasped. "I'm so sorry." *This part of the world* was barely more than a two-hour drive from her home. "Were they ever recovered?"

A slight smile frozen to her full lips, Jacinta shook her head.

The breath caught in Luz's throat and her stomach shook. "Surely not Diego…" she choked out.

"I will pray for him that it is not so."

"What do I do? I mean how do I find out?"

Jacinta shrugged. "If Diego and Pilar were taken, it is out of our hands."

"It has to be in someone's hands!" But whose?

"The Mexican government does not condone human trafficking, yet it has not been able to stop the trade. The authorities do not seem to think it merits an all-out war against the perpetrators."

"Maybe that's not it any more than drugs," Luz said, trying to be hopeful. "Maybe Pilar ran away for some totally personal reason and Diego just went after her."

"Perhaps. But you can usually reach him, yes?"

"Maybe something happened to his cell phone."

"Perhaps," Jacinta said again.

But Luz could tell the other woman wasn't convinced. "If I could look through Diego's things, I might be able to find something, some clue…" Maybe even the cell. He might have left it behind and so was unable to reach her.

After considering the request for a moment, Jacinta nodded. "I will let you into his rooms."

The climb to the fourth-floor apartment left Luz breathless. Or perhaps it wasn't the climb at all. She ran most mornings and worked out three times a week, so she had terrific stamina.

Perhaps it was the certainty that Diego was gone, taken from her as swiftly as he'd found her. She'd only learned she had a half brother a half-dozen years ago, when they'd gone to the same university. Diego had chosen the University of Texas at San Antonio purposely so that his father would have the opportunity to claim him at last. A young man's pipe dream. Instead, Luz had learned about Diego and embraced a relationship with the brother she hadn't even known existed.

Now she might have lost him forever.

THEY'D DRUGGED his food for days, maybe for weeks—he'd lost track of how long he'd been a prisoner. For most of that time, he'd forgotten who he was, how he'd gotten in this place. He'd had no will to try to get away. He'd simply survived in a vacuum.

Then one day they'd punished him for being too slow, not just with another brutal whipping, but by withholding his evening meal as well.

"Maybe an empty belly will make you work harder tomorrow, *gringo!*"

The stocky guard had kicked him and left him face-down in his cell. A chain fastened to a metal ankle bracelet had kept him anchored to the wall.

By morning, things had started coming back to him.

His name—*Quinlan McKenna Farrell.*

His job—*Special Agent for ICE, Immigrations and Customs Enforcement.*

His home—*originally a ranch in South Dakota, now an apartment in San Antonio.*

When he wasn't working undercover...

Remembering all that—and that he wasn't an animal to be forced, sometimes whipped, into doing hard labor in the fields and in the closed-off, airless building where they'd processed the plants into drugs—he'd stopped eating several days ago.

Once he'd figured it out, how they were doing this to him, he'd flushed the food down the toilet in his cell.

Once his mind had cleared completely, he'd formulated an escape plan.

The first rays of light penetrated the cell window. He could hear muffled noises and voices. They were serving breakfast to the "workers." The prisoners were bunked in small groups, none of them isolated and chained as he was. He'd noted that as he'd been brought back to his cell the last few days. The others might be physically strong men, but their wills were weak. Or maybe it was the drugs at work that depleted them mentally just as it had done to him.

Only *he* was chained to the wall like an animal.

*Not for much longer.*

Quin lay on the floor, sprawled half on his back, half on his side, as if he'd simply collapsed. He let his eyes drift next to closed, remaining open in slits just wide enough to see a slight blur through his lashes.

*The door opening...*

*Legs coming toward him...*

"Hey, *gringo,* get up and eat! You don't get no sick days here."

The guard laughed. Quin didn't respond, didn't so much

as tighten a muscle, even knowing what was coming. The toe of the guard's boot caught him in the side, hard, jerking Quin's inert body. It took all his will not to respond too soon.

And then the guard did what Quin had hoped for. He leaned forward, one hand still holding the bowl of drugged slop, the other reaching for Quin's shoulder.

"Hey, get up!"

Quin flashed his eyes open. "Okay."

And then Quin grabbed the lowered arm and pulled the guard down so fast that he didn't have time to react. The bowl flew out of his hand, and the slop flew out of the bowl to splatter the walls of the small room.

Quin wrapped the chain around the guard's neck. The other man fought it…made unintelligible noises…tried to get his fingers under the tightening vise. His fury and fear pummeled Quin, but he steadied himself against the roiling emotions. He gave the chain a sharp twist and the guard immediately went as still as a marionette whose strings were dropped.

Breathing hard, Quin needed a moment to rid himself of the dead man's effect on him. Being an empath could be a negative in his profession. He had his grandmother, Moira McKenna, to thank for what, in his mind, was a weakness he didn't need.

He steadied inside and got to work.

Hanging from the guard's belt, the keys were easy to find. The small one undid the leg iron. Next, Quin confiscated the man's weapons—two handguns and a knife—and armed himself.

After picking up the key ring, he slid to the door and listened for any other guards who might be around. Nothing. He guessed they—*El Jefe* or whoever gave orders in that bastard's stead—figured drugged men didn't need more than one guard at mealtime. Quin poked his head out, took a quick look around, then left the cell. The other prisoners were intent on their breakfast.

"Stop eating!" he whispered as he opened the first cage. "Your food is drugged."

Looking at him with half-vacant eyes, the other men kept shoveling the gruel into their mouths. Quin shook his head. He didn't think anyone understood. Still, he opened the other two doors.

"Come out. If you get by the guards, you can all go home."

"Home?" one of the men called out.

"To your women and children."

A wave of longing and desperation coming off the men suddenly struck him like a physical blow. One of the prisoners dropped a bowl and made for the door. Another followed. And another.

Quin watched in dismay. Their minds and bodies were already slowed by the new infusion of drugs. They were stumbling all over each other. He couldn't just leave them here, wherever here was. They were following him now, clumsy and noisy, murmuring the names of their loved ones. Nearly a dozen unarmed, desperate men following him...

He couldn't *leave* them.

Not now. Not when he'd opened their cages. The guards outside this hellhole were fully armed.

Quin's gut roiled and his chest tightened as he realized what he had done.

Dear God, now he was responsible for all their lives!

ALTHOUGH SHE'D BEEN in Diego's place a dozen times, Luz didn't know where to start.

"I need to get back to my shop," Jacinta said. "Let me know when you leave."

"Of course."

Luz wandered around the main room, touching the things her brother had touched, stopping at the framed photograph of the two of them together.

Even though they were only half siblings, they looked alike—blue-black hair, broad features, high cheekbones. Of course, her mother was Anglo, so while his skin was copper, hers was fair, and while his eyes were dark brown, hers were hazel. Small differences in her opinion.

Luz ran a fingertip over Diego's face and her eyes suddenly wet, wondered if she would ever be able to touch him in person again. Their father wouldn't even care, so she hadn't told him Diego was missing. Luz hadn't told Mamma, either, because she hadn't wanted to upset her.

From the desk nearby, she saw the red light of the answering machine blinking at her. More than a dozen messages. Her chest tightened as she hit play. But the messages were simply from friends who wanted Diego to call them back. No information here. What she really needed was to be able to get to his cell phone voice mail.

Opening the desk drawer, she shuffled around the papers. A couple of notes to himself—a grocery list, a phone number. Nothing to help her. Still, she checked the other drawers. The bottom one had various instruction booklets dropped into it, including the one for his cell. Luz flipped through it, to the part that told her how to retrieve voice mail messages. He'd penned in a number—7-4-5-2-7—his code?

Although she couldn't figure out why he'd chosen that particular number—it didn't correspond to his birthday or anything else familiar—she quickly tried it. Eureka! It worked. She went through Diego's messages—mostly from her begging her brother to call her. And then she went back to the saved messages.

"Diego," came a whispered voice that Luz recognized as Pilar's. "They took me across the border…"

A muffled shriek…and then the call was cut off.

Texas? That's what it sounded like, Luz thought. Talk about irony! She'd crossed into Mexico to find her brother and no doubt he was on the other side of the border trying to find Pilar!

But where in Texas?

On instinct, she decided to check Diego's computer, his e-mails. To her surprise, he'd left the computer on—it merely had been in sleep mode—and his e-mail was up. Even though she checked all the e-mails in the Inbox, Sent and Trash folders for the week since Pilar went missing, she found no clues as to Diego's whereabouts.

Discouraged, she checked the taskbar. He'd left his browser open. She checked each of the three tabs to see what he'd been reading. News on one page…weather on the second…a map on the third.

The news was an article about human trafficking. The weather was for southwestern Texas. And the map covered an area of the Rio Grande west and north of San Antonio—from just below Piedras Negras, Mexico, to just above Amistad National Recreation Area in Texas, nearly a one-hundred-mile spread. She checked the browser History and found he'd brought up the map page on the very day he'd disappeared…

Her chest went tight and she had to swallow hard to get past the lump in her throat.

Undoubtedly the map and the phone call from Pilar were connected. But how had Diego made the connection? And how could she narrow down where to look for him? A hundred miles long by who knew how many miles wide was a lot of territory to cover.

Luz put the computer back in sleep mode, grabbed her bag and turned out the apartment lights. She might as well get back to Texas as quickly as possible. Distractedly trying to figure out her next step—maybe insist her father hire a private detective—she left the apartment.

It wasn't until she reached the stairwell that she realized she wasn't alone. A scuff behind her was all the warning she got before a cloth bag was thrown over her head and before she could scream, a hand covered her mouth and she felt a sharp pinch in her arm.

And then nothing…

## Chapter Two

"Let's review what we know about this *El Jefe*."

Special Agent in Charge Maria Gonzales might have been small and slight, but her dark eyes lit with a fire that left no doubt about her passion and commitment to the job. The agents who filled the conference room of the San Antonio SAC Office of Investigation awaited her command.

"Roberto?" she asked, focusing on the agent closest to her.

"No one has ever admitted to seeing the man," he said. "His identity is well-protected. We know he's gone by the names José Estes, Pablo Arango and Arturo Fuentes, but there is no record of any of these men in south Texas at least."

Maria looked to the next agent.

"His human trafficking operation runs as far south as Guanajuato. After crossing the border it comes north through Texas and New Mexico."

As several others spoke up, Quin sat quietly at the rear of the room, just listening. So far, they hadn't revealed any information he didn't already know. In his mind, they didn't know squat. They hadn't been knocked out and dragged off to another country, been chained, intimidated and beaten. They hadn't been responsible for a dozen men being wounded or worse.

Officially, Quin was on medical leave from his job—he'd

escaped only two days ago, hardly enough time to recover from his ordeal, at least according to the shrink—but he refused to be shut out. Thankfully, whatever drugs he'd been on weren't addictive in so short time, so he was good. Maria had agreed Quin could attend the briefing as long as he remained a ghost.

"*El Jefe* owns a string of brothels all over south Texas along the border," a woman said.

Aaron Keller, Quin's partner, spoke up. "What we don't know is how far his distribution system runs."

Aaron looked like he might work in intelligence rather than in investigation, with his wiry five-ten frame encased in a designer suit, his wheat-colored hair fashioned in a precise cut around a narrow, soft-featured face. Quin knew the looks were a fooler, though. Aaron was as tough as they came, a man you wanted watching your back.

Aaron said, "We think he may be supplying brothels in California, too."

"And supplying drugs while he's at it," Quin added.

"Special Agent Farrell, you are not here," Maria reminded him.

Quin nodded but kept going. "Women aren't the only targets. Men were working the fields—"

Quin fell silent when Maria pulled her gaze from him and asked one of the other men, "How is your undercover operation going?"

Frustrated, Quin listened to the other agent's response with half an ear. Why he'd insisted on being at this meeting, he didn't know. He needed to be out in the field, working undercover himself. He needed to root out the evil known as *El Jefe* and make him pay—not only for taking him prisoner, but also for the brutality that had stopped the other men from regaining their freedom.

Unable to bear the fresh memory that seared him, Quin put it out of his mind.

If only he hadn't allowed himself to be distracted by a woman in the first place. No one had gotten closer to uncovering the identity of *El Jefe* than he had. After working undercover for months, he'd almost done it, would have done it if he hadn't been betrayed by Bianca Ramos. He'd had it all worked out—or so he'd thought—starting with her escape. And then fear had made her turn him in. Apparently she preferred continuing her life in enforced prostitution to the shot at freedom he'd offered her.

The meeting was breaking up.

Quin was the first one out the door. He went back into the bullpen and perched himself on Aaron's desk. His own desk had already been assigned to some new agent who'd been transferred in a few weeks after he'd gone missing.

*As if he really were a ghost and no longer existed…*

His best friend at the bureau, Aaron had thumped Quin on the back after he'd dragged himself in. A moment's weakness. Now Aaron was his usual no-nonsense self.

"I'm surprised." He chucked his notepad on the desk next to Quin's hip and then threw himself in his chair. "Obviously you learned self-control."

"I learned a lot of things while I was gone." Things Quin didn't want to have to face.

"You certainly look different."

Quin ran his hand over the heavy beard stubble, a reminder of the full beard he'd grown while a prisoner. "You have something against face hair?"

"Not exactly regulation."

"Maybe not for a desk job. Undercover is a different story."

"You're not undercover now, Quin. You're not even cleared to be here officially." Aaron's gaze went to the hair that hung along Quinn's face to brush his shoulders.

"I haven't exactly had time to make it to a stylist."

"The hair speaks to the real you." Aaron lifted an eyebrow as if challenging him to disagree.

Knowing it made him look a little wild—and hopefully dangerous—Quin mumbled an epithet under his breath so only Aaron would hear.

"Maybe I'll keep the look for a while. You know, like a souvenir. A reminder of where I've been for the last month." His gut clenched when he added, "Who knows how long they'll keep me in this limbo?"

A month—had he really been held for that long? It was still hard for Quin to grasp the reality. It was still hard for him to believe he was free when the other men weren't.

"Don't worry, man, the shrink will reinstate you. Eventually."

"Right."

"You *are* seeing him?"

Quin spread his hands. "Did my duty first thing this morning." He'd done his best to say all the right things, the things the shrink wanted to hear before clearing Quin.

"That must have been an early appointment. No wonder you look like hell. Go home and get some rest."

"Don't need rest."

"What do you need?" Aaron sat back in his chair and locked gazes with Quin. "Revenge?"

"That would be against the rules."

"Yeah, like that would bother you."

"I've never done anything illegal."

"Yet."

"Spit it out, Aaron. You're champing at the bit to say it, so just let it out."

"You've been skirting the rules for years, Quin. We both know that." He waited a beat, then added, "We both know that's how you got yourself in trouble."

"You think I was wrong to try to help someone?"

"That was a personal decision, not one that you made for the operation or even for the team. A wrong decision that could have cost lives. We all know it. That's why Maria is so pissed at you—because you could have gotten yourself dead. You let yourself be blinded by a pretty face."

"Maybe it wasn't her face that blinded me."

"Whatever. Your lust for the woman compromised you. Compromised the mission."

"So which was worse? In your opinion."

Not that mere lust had reeled him in. He had slept with Bianca to get the information he needed and had been sucked in by his own plan. Being an empath, he'd been reeled in by the strong emotions he'd felt from her, so when she'd asked if he could help free her from this life that had been forced on her, what was he to think? His McKenna heritage made him a sucker to emotion—if he didn't concentrate and turn it off, he felt everything others did—and Bianca had blasted him with her panicky, confusing thinking.

How could he have known that in the end, she would choose to protect herself by betraying him?

The irony was that she'd done it on his thirty-third birthday. The very birthday in which he was supposed to find his true love if his grandmother's personal legacy to her grandchildren was to be believed. Considering what had happened to him, the very idea made him want to laugh.

"So what are you going to do now?" Aaron asked.

"What? You don't think I'm going to go home like a good dog until some shrink pats me on the head and deems me fit to do my job?"

Aaron shook his head. "I didn't think so."

"Would *you*?"

"I don't know. What you've been through—"

"I'm fine."

"You don't look fine."

"So you already told me."

"I don't mean the stubble or the hair. It's your eyes, man." Aaron locked gazes with him and stared with intensity. "I keep looking in there, trying to find the Special Agent Quinlan McKenna Farrell I know and…" He shook his head. "He's…well, he's just missing."

Even though Quin wanted to look away, he kept his gaze steady. So what if everything he'd gone through had changed him. How could it not? It simply made him stronger. A special agent with even more purpose.

"I'm fine, Aaron. Ready to get back on the job. To go after *El Jefe* full force."

"You need time."

"The longer I wait, the harder it'll be to come back."

"Maybe that would be a good thing. Maybe you'd look at the job differently with some distance."

"Or maybe not at all. Maybe I would just get the hell out of Dodge. I've got a ranch to go back to in South Dakota. And people. Parents. A sister and brother. In-laws I've never met." Even when he wasn't in direct touch, he kept track of what was going on back home. Or had until he'd become obsessed with this mission. "For all I know, I could be an uncle a couple times over by now."

"You weren't gone that long."

"I've been gone longer than you imagine, at least to my family."

He'd been living life on the edge for so long with his under-cover assignments that he hadn't felt right contacting them, drawing them into his murky world. Although one of his siblings or cousins might have some inkling given their psychic inheritance from their grandmother. Dreams…vision through touch…an unearthly connection with animals. It was different for each of the nine cousins.

Quin seemed to have gotten a little of everything, just like his Grandmother Moira. Only unlike his grandmother, he'd never truly appreciated his gifts, had never really made them work for him. He'd spent more time covering up so he wouldn't be considered a freak.

Maybe it was time to change all that.

"My being gone just wasn't official until I got railroaded into Mexico to do slave labor like some kind of zombie."

"So what are you going to do about it?" Aaron asked again. "You know whatever you decide, I'm there."

"Thanks."

Quin really meant it, even though he didn't want to involve his friend deeply enough to get him into trouble if things went bad again.

Aaron sighed with resignation. "What are you planning?"

"I thought I could use some recreation." Quin's grin was humorless as he said, "A woman."

"One of *El Jefe's* bordellos?" Aaron snapped.

"Why not?"

"Which one?"

"Haven't decided yet. Maybe I'll ask for a virgin. Undoubtedly I can get a girl who'll be underage as well as an illegal and I'll be able to make an arrest with some serious time behind it."

Hopefully the woman who ran the brothel would look out for herself and betray her employer as quickly as Bianca Ramos had betrayed him. And this time, he would look more closely on anything revealed to him through his psychic powers. Not that he would tell Aaron that. He was careful to keep his abilities to himself.

"Are you crazy, Quin? You're not on active duty."

"But I'm a man who needs recreation. To relax. It's only

natural I would want a woman after all this time. If I happen into a situation that's illegal, it's still my duty to do something about it."

Aaron groaned. "You're going to get us both kicked out of the department."

Quin realized he was being unfair. "I'll leave you out of it, then."

"No! If you're going in, then I want to know your every move."

"Maybe that's not such a good idea. You have your family to think about." Something Quin wished he could claim. "You don't need to worry about losing your job—"

"It's either worry about the job or worry about you," Aaron argued. "If you're going to do this, then you better damn well tell me everything! But why can't you just be patient? Give yourself time to heal! A few days, maybe a few weeks, and the shrink will clear you for active duty. Then you can do this through channels."

A shrink couldn't give him absolution for the men who'd been hurt or killed because of him. He only knew he needed to act so that what had happened at the labor camp couldn't happen to anyone else.

"Channels don't work fast enough for me. I want someone to know I'm going in—I could use backup—but I *am* going in, whether or not I have it."

"You think I would let you down?" Aaron groaned and cursed under his breath. "You know I have your back, Quin! Just go easy this time. Be careful, for God's sake. And whatever else you do, resist temptation. Don't get yourself mixed up with another woman!"

"So you weren't lying, after all." Speaking to Luz in Spanish, the little rotund man who called himself a doctor snapped off his latex gloves. "You really are a virgin. That increases your value."

Luz nearly choked on a sob. "Please, this is a mistake. I'm an American citizen. Please help me get to my consulate and let them get me back to my own country."

He untied her and then left the horrid little windowless room without so much as another word to her. The walls felt like they were closing in on her as she got off the makeshift examination table. That and a cart with medical supplies and the wooden chair holding the armed guard were the only furnishings in the room.

Luz shook as she pulled on a T-shirt left at the end of the table. They hadn't even given her the privacy of a paper gown. She'd lain there, nude, half-drugged and fully tied down as she'd been checked inside out, an armed guard in the room laughing as she'd begged the doctor to please stop, to please help her.

To at least tell her where she was and what they wanted of her.

As if she didn't know.

The masks of the missing women in the shop belonging to Diego's landlady suddenly clear in her mind, she wondered if her face would join the "Missing" on the wall.

The guard was still there, his expression lascivious as his gaze roamed over every inch of her skin. He stroked his gun and grunted at her. Alarmed, she turned her back to him to pull on the knit shorts, stumbling a little as she clumsily tried to get her foot through the opening that seemed to keep moving. All the while, she could feel his obscene interest in her.

Her skin crawled in response.

Hanging on to the examination table, she managed to get the shorts on, then slipped her feet into slides that were a little tight. She stood there, mortified at the things that had happened to her the last few days and wondered what they were going to do with her now.

Whoever *they* were.

The guard grunted at her and opened the door, wielding his weapon at the opening, indicating she should leave the room.

"Where are you taking me?"

No surprise that he didn't answer.

As she walked down the hall, she heard other voices. More Spanish.

"Dr. Herrera assures me she's a virgin," a woman was saying.

"Then prepare her properly, Maribel. Most of the virgins brought in are cattle."

"This one has looks."

"Then play them up. Make sure she knows what to do. Maybe then she'll be worth more than the thousand we usually get for a first time."

The guard shoved her through the door at the man and woman discussing her fate.

The man—distinguished in a designer suit, a single thick streak of silver in his glossy dark hair—looked her over, nodded. "We'll ask for two thousand." Then left.

Maribel was middle-aged but still beautiful, even if she wore too much makeup and a too-short, too-tight red dress that would have suited someone with a younger, slimmer body. She was plush, if not truly overweight. Her hair was cut short, her nails were long and polished the same red as the dress.

Maribel waved the guard away and said, "Your name?"

"Luz…Lucille…I'm Lucille Delgado from San Antonio, Texas. Help me, please. If it's money you want, I can get it for you—"

Maribel laughed. "I know you can. And you will. But first we have to get you looking like something a man would want to take to his bed."

Luz tried in vain to get Maribel to listen to reason. The woman forced her into a bathroom and told her to get herself clean or she would do it for Luz.

A half hour later, every inch of her skin scrubbed and now wrapped in a satin robe, her hair washed and dried, Luz was led from the bathroom up two flights of dimly lit stairs.

"You're a virgin, but you're not so young, so I expect you have some idea of what to do with a man."

"I'm twenty-eight." And she really had no concrete idea—her experience being limited mostly to romance novels and movies.

Maribel stopped and laughed. "What are you, a nun? A twenty-eight-year-old virgin? Impossible."

"I assure you it's not."

"You'll say you're twenty and they'll believe you. No man would want an old virgin." Maribel led the way into a hallway. "You'll be quiet and watch."

"Watch what?"

Maribel hissed at her and put her finger to her lips. Then she stopped in front of what looked like a window, but on the other side of the glass was a bedroom. Not empty. A paunchy, middle-aged man was lying on the bed with his pants dropped to his knees. A beautiful young woman bent over him and drew him into her mouth.

Luz looked away, but with a clawed hand on Luz's neck, Maribel shoved her face back around to the window and whispered into her ear. "Watch how talented she is. You need to be good at pleasuring a man like this."

*This* didn't take long. The middle-aged man bucked and shouted and Luz thought her humiliation was now complete.

Not so.

Maribel took her from window to window, bedroom to bedroom, and threatened her if she didn't watch and learn.

Most of what she saw was unexceptional and she put her mind in limbo until they came to the window where a client was abusing a girl—slapping her even as he rode her.

"Aren't you going to do something? He's hurting her."

"Because she hasn't learned her job well enough. Or because she hasn't made him believe she loves what he's doing to her. What the client wants is everything."

A sense of unreality, the feeling that she was stuck in a nightmare, filled her. "You have to stop this."

"I don't have to do anything but make sure my clients get their money's worth. Just remember what you see here when you meet your first client. If you don't please him, don't work hard enough, this could be you."

The statement was enough to put an additional layer of fear in Luz's heart. Any curiosity she'd had about sex was now dead. She didn't care if she never experienced the supposed pleasures of the flesh.

This wasn't going to happen to her. None of this. She would rather die first.

That thought uppermost in her mind, she let Maribel, obviously the madam of this establishment, lead her to a dressing room where she prodded, poked and stuffed Luz into a tantalizing see-through flesh-colored piece of lingerie that pulled in her waist and pushed her breasts up so they looked ripe to spill from the top. She might as well be nude, Luz thought. Parts of her were. Maribel gave her a cover-up that did little to make her feel better. And strappy platform sandals with four-inch heels made her feel worse. Then the madam curled and styled her dark red-brown hair in an intricate up-do and applied layers of makeup, instructing her to watch carefully so she could do it for herself the next time.

"The client wants you to please him like a whore while

looking like an angel," Maribel said before leaving her alone with her racing thoughts.

What she looked like was a prostitute.

Staring into the mirror, Luz truly didn't recognize herself. Maybe that was just as well. She could pretend she was someone other than Luz Delgado. She didn't know how long she sat like that—kohl-rimmed eyes wide, mind in a dark place—before Maribel returned.

"It's time."

"No!" Luz shook her head. "I can't do this!"

"You can and you will. I knew I should have given you drugs. It's not too late—"

"No, please, no more drugs." Luz moved to the other woman. Drugs would cloud her mind again and then she never would find an escape.

Maribel nodded. "Fine, let's go. You'll meet your client in the honeymoon suite. You'll do whatever he wants. Give him whatever he wants. You'll make him the most satisfied man on earth. Do you understand?"

"Yes, I understand what you want." Let her take that as an agreement. She had to find a way out of this! "Will you be watching me, too?"

"No, only certain clients pay extra for the excitement of being watched. But your date for the night will certainly complain if you disappoint him."

*Clients paid to be watched?*

Disgusting as the idea was, Luz breathed a little easier. No one would be watching *her*. Maybe she could reason with the client, assure him that if he helped her get free of the place and got her home, Pappa would reward him well. Pay him double or triple what he paid for her services. Luz was financially comfortable, but Pappa was a very wealthy big rancher. And he would do anything for one of his daughters.

She pushed aside the memory of his disapproval over her chasing after her brother. Pappa would never hold that against her, not in a situation like this. He would simply be grateful to see her returned home safely.

It was her only hope. If only they would leave her alone for a while, she would try to escape now that her head was clear of the drugs. But security guards seemed to be everywhere. Luz suspected she wouldn't be left alone. And she wouldn't be surprised if there were bars on the damn windows!

Maribel stopped at the hand-carved double doors and said, "Don't disappoint me."

Nodding, Luz swallowed hard and stepped inside and listened to the doors close behind her. The room was cool, the light dim. She got the impression of a four-poster bed with mirrors on the ceiling and an imposing silhouette of her client looking out a window.

He was tall with broad shoulders and a slim waist. Not at all built like the clients she'd been forced to spy on earlier. When he turned, her stomach fluttered and then knotted. Shoulder-length black hair framed a beard-stubbled face which was drawn into an expression she could only describe as brutish. His blue eyes narrowed on her and his right cheek twitched so that she could see the shiny scar beneath the stubble.

"Dance for me, darlin'," he said smoothly in Spanish. "Show me what you got."

## Chapter Three

As sultry as the mahogany-haired woman who entered the room turned out to be, Quin could see she wasn't some underage virgin. No virgin looked like that—full breasts, narrow waist, shapely hips all enhanced by the cut of the skimpy garment she wore. The shadow of her nipples and the dark V nestled at her thighs made his groin tighten, so he focused on her face, painted and outlined with too much makeup. A smear of red gloss emphasized the shape of her full lips, thick lines of charcoal the slant of her hazel eyes, a burst of blush the fullness of her broad cheekbones.

Hell was a cold place if this was a virgin!

Angry that he'd been thwarted—he'd hoped to make an immediate arrest and start the downward spiral of *El Jefe's* human trafficking operation—he stood his ground, waiting to see what she was going to do.

She certainly didn't dance.

She didn't even move, just stood there, staring at him with those big eyes. Staring at him like she was afraid of what a man could give her.

Another Bianca, he thought, sly and willing to play-act if it would be to her benefit.

Or perhaps they had threatened her.

Well, he could still turn this around. She didn't have to be an underage virgin to help him close this place down. She merely had to be willing to testify that this bordello was selling her wares, therefore making money illegally. Shutting down one bordello would barely make a dent in *El Jefe's* operation, but it was a start. Quin intended to chip away at the tentacles until he caught *El Jefe's* attention.

And if she didn't cooperate…intimidation usually worked.

He stalked across the room, his gaze pinning the woman in place. She blinked and a small moan escaped her. He grinned at her and her eyes went even wider. She backed up…almost tripped…grabbed on to the bedpost to save herself from falling off those platform shoes.

He snaked a hand up her bare arm to her shoulder and froze. Fear leeched off her. No, something a bit more complex. Add a dash of disgust. For him?

He got the distinct feeling she didn't want to be here with him and was looking for a way out.

Virgin or not, she was his only resource. As intimidated as she seemed to be, maybe it wouldn't be so hard to get what he needed from her, after all.

"You don't seem like the typical who…um, woman who ends up in a place like this."

Her distrust suddenly washed over him.

Did she suspect why he was here? Or had someone else? Had she been warned?

He slid his hand over the smooth hot skin of her shoulder— she shuddered and he could sense her tightening inside— stopping only when his fingers lightly encircled her neck.

"Are you really going to h-hurt me?" she gasped.

Staring deep into her defiant eyes, he tilted his head closer so that his breath brushed her cheek. "Why would you think that? Have you done something that will make me angry?"

"No!"

Her fear was growing into terror, and Quin sensed he was missing something. He was playing with her, not pushing her that hard. He let go of her neck and backed off.

"Then why are you so afraid of me?" he asked.

"I-I shouldn't be here. They took me…brought me here, wherever this is!" she choked out, her words stumbling one over the other. "I need help to get away from this place, but I don't know how or where I can go. Will you help me, please? I can make it worth your while."

Suddenly he sensed the terror receding a bit, as hope warred with her darker emotions.

So either she *was* a victim of *El Jefe's* human trafficking operation or she was an even better actress than Bianca, who'd pretty much given him the same line.

"Why should I believe you?" he demanded. "Who brought you here?"

"I don't know. M-my brother disappeared and I was looking for him at his apartment in Nuevo Laredo. When I c-came out, I realized someone was behind me…" She shuddered. "They threw something over my head and then drugged me, so I never saw them. I just want to go home, back to Texas. My father will reward you well for helping me."

Quin started. She was serious. She thought she was still in Mexico. He began to relax. Began to believe her. While she spoke perfect Spanish, her accent didn't seem quite right. Still, he wasn't going to make it too easy for her.

He switched to English. "I'll help you if you'll help me."

"Me help *you*? To do what?"

She'd also switched to English, spoken without the slightest Mexican accent. If anything, she sounded Southern. She must be Texan, all right.

"Where did you say you were from?" he asked.

"San Antonio."

Hell, they could be neighbors for all he knew.

"What are you fixin' to do?" Luz asked. "What do you think I can do to help you?"

"You can agree to testify in a court of law."

LUZ STARTED. This was going too fast for her. First she thought this man was going to hurt her. Then he'd backed off, started speaking to her in English.

Now he wanted her to agree to…what?

"What are you talking about?" she asked.

"When I bring the owner of this brothel before a judge, I want to make sure you'll testify, tell the judge what happened to you."

Trying to get her thoughts together, Luz blinked at him silently for a moment before demanding, "Just who the hell are you?"

"I work for ICE—Immigrations and Customs Enforcement." When she didn't immediately respond, he explained, "I'm working undercover. Special Agent Quinlan McKenna Farrell with the Office of Investigation. I'm here to close down this place."

"You have identification?"

Slipping a leather ID holder out of the top of his boot, he showed it to her.

How did she know he was for real? People could get fake IDs, even ones that identified them as government agents. She didn't have a clue what an ICE identification would look like in the first place. She had to admit the badge looked pretty real. Not knowing why someone would pretend to be an ICE agent and considering her circumstances, Luz decided to go with the hope that he really could rescue her.

"So why is someone from U.S. Immigrations and Customs working in Mexico?" As far as she knew, he had no powers here.

"We're not in Mexico. We're in Texas."

"What? Where?"

"At a ranch along the Rio Grande, an hour or so from San Antonio."

Luz sank down into a nearby chair. "Omigod, they got me across the border. But how?"

"Were you drugged?"

She nodded, "Yes, drugged. And tied and blindfolded. All I remember is being thrown into a vehicle…and then nothing. When I came to, I was here."

"Smuggled in, maybe even across one of the international bridges in the back of a van."

Is that what had happened to Pilar? In the message on her brother's answering machine, Pilar had said she'd been taken across the border. What if she was here, in this place?

"So, let me get this straight, you go into brothels and shut them down?"

"Not specifically. I work undercover to break up human trafficking rings. I'm trying to get the goods on a creep who goes by the moniker *El Jefe*. He runs a big operation. Women disappear off the streets of Mexico and end up in places like this all through south Texas."

"How many places?"

"We don't know the extent of his network for sure. At least a handful, probably more. And then there are the women who don't have the looks to fit these accommodations but still serve their purpose being sold out of trailers where there are migrant workers. And other women are put to work in like situations in New Mexico and California."

Luz shook her head. "I don't understand how something like this can happen in this country."

"The strong have always preyed on the weak. Money is power and a lot of people who don't have either want both." He shifted gears, asking, "So…what is *your* name?"

"Luz Delgado."

"Call me Quin." He held out a hand. "Do we have a deal, Luz?"

Reluctantly she shook. Although she wasn't a small woman, her hand was nearly engulfed by his. He was a very big man. Not just tall, but wide, looking like his shoulders could nearly fill a doorway.

"Can I count on you to help me?" he asked.

"Of course. Whatever it takes. But first things first. How are you going to get me out of here?"

"I have a plan. Let's go see the madam." Then he told her how they could get a quick audience. "Be uncooperative. Now scream," he ordered, pulling her up from the chair. "And fight me like you mean it." When she didn't immediately do as he asked, he pulled her against him. "Scream if you don't want to end up in that bed."

Not knowing if he meant with him or with some other man, Luz screamed for all she was worth.

Quin grinned at her. "Good. Now let's put on a big, noisy show." Throwing open the door, he exited, dragging her by the wrist while shouting in Spanish. "You're coming with me! I paid good money for you and I intend to get my money's worth!"

"Let go of me! I'm not for sale!"

Luz fought Quin like the scenario was real. He didn't so much as flinch when she smacked him. He merely pulled her to him and snaked an arm around her to secure her.

"We'll see about that," he muttered as a fresh-faced kid wearing a tan and brown security guard uniform stepped in front of them.

His fingers brushing the gun at his side, the young guard demanded, "What are you doing?"

Struggling to get out Quin's grasp, Luz grew breathless. "He's trying to force me to—"

Her accusation was cut off when Quin covered her mouth with his free hand. She didn't stop struggling. He kept up the act, didn't let her get the edge. As far as she was concerned, he didn't have to be quite so convincing!

"Going to see Maribel," Quin said. "Either she gets this whore to work or I get my money back."

Appearing nervous, the guard said, "Wait back in your room. I'll tell Señora Maribel you want to talk to her."

"You're not tryin' to stop me, are you?" Quin yelled, looking down his nose at the smaller man. "Because that would just make me madder!"

The way the guard was fiddling with the handle of his gun made Luz nervous.

"Please, your voice…you'll disturb the other clients. I can't let you wander around alone—"

"Then take me to her yourself."

Luz let go a yell of triumph, which was muffled behind Quin's hand. He looked down at her and winked, reminding her their struggle was for show. Having nearly exhausted herself, certain she would need any reserves she had to actually get out of this place, she merely cursed him in Spanish, hoping the guard would get the gist of her muted words and keep believing in their act.

Quin dragged her along, practically carrying her down the staircase and across the foyer to the front parlor. Inside, women lounged in various states of undress. Luz took a good look at them all. Most chatted away as if they were okay with their profession. But one sat at the window, looking out as if with longing. And another was folded into herself in a corner.

She simply looked drugged. But none of them were Diego's girlfriend.

Still Luz wondered if these women were prisoners just as she was. Not for long. Quin would have to get them out of there as well. Surely he wouldn't leave other victims behind.

The guard brought them through the room straight to an office in the back.

Sitting behind the desk, a ledger open before her, Maribel immediately looked up at the interruption. "What is going on here?"

Quin pushed the guard aside and with a nod of his shaggy head indicated the man should leave. "Get out. My business isn't with you."

The madam waved him off and gave Luz a dark look. "What has she done?" Then she locked gazes with Luz. "I told you what was expected of you and what would happen to you if you didn't cooperate."

At that, Quin let go of Luz and changed his demeanor. "You're not going to do anything to her. Do you realize you've abducted and illegally transported a U.S. citizen across the border?"

Her expression outraged, Maribel demanded, "Who do you think you are?"

He pulled out his ID and threw it on the desk in front of her. "If you're as smart as I think you are, you'll cooperate with my investigation."

Maribel started to touch the ID, then pulled her hands back and slid them under the desk. "What is this?"

"It's an arrest," he informed her. "If you cooperate, give up *El Jefe*, I can probably get you a deal. No jail time. Sound good?"

"Who is *El Jefe*?"

"As if you didn't know...the man who runs this operation."

"*I* run this operation."

"You're nothing but the madam."

Luz suddenly spoke up. "When I got here, she was taking

orders from some oily-looking older guy in an expensive suit. He has a big, thick streak of silver in his hair. Maybe he's this *El Jefe*."

"I don't know what you're talking about," Maribel said, her voice tight.

Quin moved in on her, stuck his beard-stubbled face over the desk. "Do you think he would appreciate your sacrificing yourself for him? I'm closing you down and taking you in. You'd do best to cooperate."

Fury crossed Maribel's features, but she quickly composed herself before saying, "I don't think so."

"What makes you so confident?"

"They do."

A superior smile etched on her face, she nodded to the doorway behind him as the young security guard rushed in, followed by two others who looked older, bigger and definitely meaner.

"Did you think I wasn't ready for you? Take them and lock them up!" Maribel shouted the command with confidence.

Then Quin growled, "I don't think so."

# Chapter Four

Luz watched wide-eyed as Quin whirled around, picked up the young guard and threw him against the other two so all three went stumbling back into the parlor. Guard number two pulled his gun. Quin kicked his arm so that the gun went spinning, only to be tackled by number three and thrown into the middle of the room.

What now? What could she do? Luz wondered.

She went for the discarded gun.

"Get it before she does!"

The screeched order from Maribel drove one of the prostitutes to beat her to it. Luz found herself in a tug-of-war over the weapon with an equally scantily-clad woman. Using her superior size and strength, she knocked the other woman to the floor and dropped herself on top. The prostitute swore at her like a sailor, but she let go of the gun.

Luz grabbed the weapon and got back on her feet, saying, "Don't try anything. I know how to use this."

Not that she'd had a gun in hand lately. But Pappa had taught her how to shoot when she was a kid.

She glanced over to the men. Quin backed toward the windows as the downed guards got to their feet.

Seeing an opening, she yelled, "Quin!" and tossed the gun between the guards to him.

He caught it with ease and flipped it around to grip the handle, then moved the barrel from one guard to the other. "Who should I shoot first?"

The young guard backed off immediately, then bolted from the room with Maribel screeching after him. "You're a dead man, you coward!"

Luz gained sympathy for the guy. He was probably a dead man but didn't know it yet.

That left two men, only one with a gun.

"There are two of you." Even though agitated, Maribel didn't leave the doorway, as if she meant to take shelter back in her office if things went south. "Take care of him!"

The men looked at each other—neither chose to move with Quin pointing a gun at them.

"Luz." Quin nodded his head toward the door.

They both began carefully moving in that direction while keeping the guards in check. From the corner of her eye, Luz saw a movement and whipped around to see the prostitute getting to her feet, her stance aggressive.

"I wouldn't if I were you," Luz said coolly, fixing the other woman with a warning expression.

The woman fumed but didn't move.

Then she and Quin were at the door.

"You go first—the black SUV to the right."

"What about the other women? The ones in the window and corner—" Neither had moved. "I'm sure they're prisoners."

"We're going to be lucky if I can get *us* out."

"We can't just leave them!"

"We'll send someone back for them. I promise."

Luz didn't hesitate any longer. She was out the door and running until she realized she would break her neck in the four-inch heels Maribel had made her wear. She stopped to remove them and noted there was more than one SUV among the vehicles. She checked the plates and figured the one that read QMCKF33 belonged to Quin. Grabbing the shoes, she ran. She was almost to the passenger door when Quin caught up to her.

Gunfire followed them.

Quin tackled her and pulled her around to the rear, using the vehicle as a shield. He carefully aimed and let off a couple shots himself. A yelp and Spanish curse told her he'd hit someone.

"Just a flesh wound," he muttered. "Probably won't stop him for long. If we get away his punishment might be worse than being shot again." He opened the driver's door. "Go in this way and climb over the seat. I'll cover you."

Luz climbed in to the sound of gunfire coming from both directions, but before she could get to the passenger seat, a weird noise was followed by the SUV tipping forward on the driver's side.

"Damn! He got a tire!" Quin growled. "Get out now."

Luz scrambled back toward him, at the last minute noting the man's work shirt tossed in back. She grabbed it and slid out, then dropped her shoes so she could pull on the shirt.

"What are you doing?" he asked over the sound of metallic pings.

"If you think I'm going to keep running around next-to-naked, you have another think coming."

She barely got both arms into the sleeves, when Quin grabbed a hand and started running, practically dragging her behind him, staying low and zigzagging between cars, the fireworks following.

"Hey, my shoes!"

"Shouldn't have taken them off!"

*And he was running away from the other vehicles.*

"Where are you going?" she cried when she saw the fenced-in horse pasture ahead. A hundred yards off, a pair of horses were munching contentedly, apparently unaware of the approaching danger. "Can't you hot-wire one of these other vehicles?"

Ignoring her, he kept going. Trying to fight him was an exercise in futility. If she wasn't so out of breath, she would have argued. Instead, deciding to wait for a debate she could win, she caved. A moment later they were at a fence and he was pushing her in front of him.

"Go through."

Luz slipped between ragged boards, feeling one scrape her thigh as she dropped to the other side. Looking down, she saw she was bleeding, but only a little.

Quin squeezed through after her. "We gotta move fast, before he finishes reloading."

"I don't even have shoes."

"I wasn't thinking of walking."

He set his focus on the grazing horses and whistled. Their ears twitched and their heads came up.

"What are you doing?" Luz asked.

As Quin whistled in a specific pattern of sounds that he repeated several times, he seemed to be in some kind of trance. Responding, the horses began picking their way to them.

He grabbed Luz's arm and began tugging again. When this was over, one arm was sure to be longer than the other.

He said, "I hope you know how to ride."

"Of course I know how to ride. I'm a Texan, born on a ranch. I was raised on horses."

"Bareback?"

"As a kid."

"Without a bit and reins?"

"As a kid," Luz said again, not quite so sure of herself. She'd managed it somehow, but that had been in a corral when Pappa had been giving her a lesson on how to use her legs, not her hands, to get a horse to do what she wanted.

"Let's hope your memory serves you."

Stopping next to a black and white Paint, he patted the mare and spoke quietly, too low for her to hear, then cradled his hands together to give her a leg up. She grabbed the mare's mane, set her bare foot in his cupped hands, bounced up and threw her free leg over the broad back.

Quin practically flew onto a red and white Appaloosa gelding in one big, smooth movement. He whistled again and dug his heels into the horse's sides. His mount took off and loped across the field, hers following. All she could do was hold on and try to keep her seat.

A few shots followed them, then nothing. No doubt the guard went to get a vehicle.

Where did Quin think they were going to take the horses where a four-wheel drive couldn't also go? More immediately, how did he think they were going to get out of the fenced pasture? She didn't see a gate anywhere.

Quin leaned over his horse. He was talking to the animal again. What? Did he think the horse actually understood him?

And why was he heading straight for a part of the fence that needed repair? The top board had broken and half was gone.

Quin didn't slow.

"I hope you're not planning to go over that!" she yelled.

"Hold on!" He goosed the gelding's side and leaned over its neck.

Apparently he *was* planning to do it.

Luz hadn't jumped a horse since she was a kid. Then she'd taken every challenge she could find riding out on the Delgado land. But this was crazy!

Glancing back, she saw a trail of dust circling the pasture. The guard was driving on the adjoining road like a bat out of hell, trying to head them off. Taking a deep breath, watching

Quin's mount take the jump easily, she straightened her seat, leaned over the mare's neck and held on.

She'd always thought jumping was like being on a roller coaster ride. That had never been truer as it was now. Her stomach led the way over the fence and tumbled back inside her only when they landed.

The vehicle was approaching but they left the road, headed through scrub and finally maneuvered into some brush which eventually led to trees and then a creek wide enough and deep enough to prevent any vehicle from following. Their mounts plunged through the water. Landing on the other side, they didn't stop.

Quin pushed the horses for a while longer before slowing some to give them a chance to cool out.

Luz pulled alongside him. "We were just lucky to find an area where the security guard couldn't follow. Although nothing is to say he won't find us yet."

"Luck had nothing to do with it. I knew where to go."

"What did you do? Lay out an escape route before coming into the brothel?"

"Nope." He indicated the gelding. "I asked him. He's been out this way lots of times."

Luz rolled her eyes and was about to make a sarcastic comment when she noted Quin's expression. The man was dead serious.

As if hearing her unexpressed doubts, he said, "A little gift I inherited from my Irish grandmother. Moira McKenna was known as a *bean feasa*—a woman with powers, psychic and otherwise. Communicating with animals was one of her gifts."

Not knowing how to respond to that, Luz let it go. However he'd gotten them out, she could only be grateful. But now she viewed Quin with a slightly jaundiced eye. A man who talked to animals…and who thought they spoke to him…who had she gotten herself mixed up with?

The only person willing to help her, she admitted. Crazy or not, he was her only hope of getting out of this situation in one piece.

Eventually, they came to a wider branch of the creek, its banks lined with pecan and elm and giant oak trees. There they dismounted and watered their horses.

Luz got down on the bank and drank, too, after which she tried washing off as much makeup as possible. She'd love to strip off Quin's shirt and climb into the cold water and wash away the last days. Only imagining what she'd look like if the see-through material of her lingerie got wet, she took a pass on that one.

Sticking her bare, abused feet in the water, she sighed and closed her eyes for a moment. How had she gotten herself into this mess? What had she been thinking? She should have asked Pappa to get help, should have insisted on it. What made her think she could do anything for anyone, especially when there would be potential violence? She was best at protecting herself by hiding from life.

Finally realizing she couldn't stay with her toes in the water all day, she washed off the scrape on her thigh and got to her feet.

Quin was staring at her, but she found his expression unreadable.

"Um, did I remove most of the crud from my face?"

"Most," he agreed, then before she knew what he was up to, cupped her cheek and used his thumb to brush the area below her left eye.

His touch was light, his gaze roaming her face. The way he was looking at her—like he'd never seen her before and liked what he saw now—made her squirm inside.

"Thanks."

A little breathless, Luz took a step back and used the collar of the shirt she was wearing to finish the job.

Quin turned away from her, saying, "We should take a break while I call for backup."

"Break? You think these two…" She indicated the horses. "…are just going to wait around until we're ready to go?"

"They'll keep themselves occupied grazing."

"They'll wander off."

He shrugged. "They'll come back when I call them."

Worried that might not happen, Luz wanted in the worst way to get on her mare and ride off without him. But after the way the horses had been ridden, they needed a rest. Trusting that Quin could actually call them back if they wandered off—he'd gotten them to come to him in the pasture, after all—Luz tried to relax while Quin tried to place a call on his cell.

"Damn, no signal! If I could get through, Aaron could pin down our location through the GPS." He walked around a hundred yards in each direction, before finally giving up. Flipping the cell closed, he slipped it into his pocket. "I guess we find the way home ourselves."

"For a while longer, at least. You're bound to get a signal eventually."

"I'll get a signal later when we get out of here."

The question was—how did he know where *here* was? The sun already set and when dusk fell, which was anytime now, they would be totally disoriented.

Surely he didn't mean to travel in unknown wilderness in the dark.

THEY'D traveled as far as they could go for one day—weaving in and out of a couple of small canyons—and still no signal on

Quin's cell. Afraid if he pressed it, he would run out of battery, he'd turned it off for the night when they'd made camp.

Now they sat before a campfire he'd made of mesquite branches. The smell of the burning wood got to him, reminded him of the days he and his siblings would camp out for the night on ranch land and cook over a fire.

Luz had to be starving, but she hadn't complained. To his amazement, she hadn't complained about anything. Barefooted and nearly naked, she'd shown what she was made of—the same tough fiber that was the core of the McKenna women, going back to his grandmother Moira.

She had the same heart, too, going in search of her brother alone when he'd gone missing.

Quin didn't want to think too closely on her good points. Gazing at her sitting across from him, her arms wrapped around her knees, her gaze fixed on the fire, he felt stirrings he wanted to deny. He needed to keep her a stranger, keep his head about him. But he couldn't help himself. He wanted to know what made her tick.

"You and your brother must be really close."

"Couldn't get closer," she said. "We've only known each other for six years but—"

"Whoa. Back up. How is that possible?"

"Diego's my half brother. I grew up not knowing about him. Pappa is a loving man, but he's also difficult. Diego was his mistake. He's cared for him all his life financially, but never emotionally. Pappa never wanted us to know about his out-of-wedlock son."

"Rough."

"Especially on Diego. He came to San Antonio to go to school, thinking he could make Pappa want to get to know him."

"But it didn't work?"

Luz shook her head. "If he hadn't tried, I might never have

met my own brother. He and I bonded from the moment we set eyes on each other. My sister, Natalie, accepts Diego, but she's not as close to him as I am."

Quin frowned. "I don't get it. In this day and age, lots of people have kids out of wedlock. Is your father really embarrassed by his son?"

"Not the way you think. Diego is Mexican and Pappa's family has been in Texas since before it became a state. He wants his family to be all American. He even married an Anglo and wouldn't hear Spanish spoken in the house when I was growing up."

"So he doesn't speak Spanish?"

"Of course he does. Mamma, too. He wouldn't let my sister and me learn the language—I had to wait until I went to college to explore my own heritage. Mamma never agreed with Pappa's obsession with assimilating. And when she learned about Diego, she couldn't forgive Pappa—not for having a son by another woman but for denying him. If she could've, she would have made Diego part of our family, but Pappa wanted no part of that plan. Mamma still hasn't made peace with that."

"Your mother sounds like an extraordinary woman."

"She is. I get my strength from her."

Having come from a close-knit family, Quin couldn't imagine excluding blood, no matter what. He and Kate and Neil were full blooded siblings, but his cousin Donovan had been born out of wedlock. Even so, Donovan was close to his half siblings Skelly and Aileen. And to their father, who had always tried to make them get along. The McKennas were an inclusive bunch. He imagined that if they even suspected someone was related to them, they would circle the wagons to make that person feel wanted.

"In the morning, I'll get us out of here," Quin promised her.

"We'll get to a place where the cell will work and we'll be rescued. You'll be home by tomorrow night."

"I don't want to go home, not without knowing what happened to Diego."

She'd told him about Diego's girlfriend disappearing first, about Diego going after her and subsequently disappearing. Quin didn't want to tell her that Diego could be dead. An awful thought, but the probability was high.

"I begged him to let the authorities handle it," Luz said softly, her words sounding choked, "but he said nothing would be done about a girl who wasn't related to someone of importance."

Quin figured Diego had been right. He could tell Luz was trying not to cry. If she did, who could blame her, after what she'd been through over the last few days? He wanted to reassure her in some way.

"I'll find out what happened to your brother and his girlfriend, Luz. It might take some time, but—"

"Do you really think I can just go back to my old life like nothing happened? If they hadn't brought me to you—" She shuddered.

"But you're all right now."

"I'll never be all right. Not until the animals who did this are shut down. Not until I see Diego and Pilar with my own eyes and know they are safe. I will do anything I have to, Quin…anything. I should have told Pappa and begged him to hire professionals…or at least I should have gone to the authorities. I was reckless and wasted precious time…and now I feel responsible for what happens to my brother."

Quin didn't argue. He didn't tell her that her brother might already be dead. That her brother's woman might wish she *was* dead. He couldn't tell her that they might never find out what happened to them.

He couldn't take away her hope.

He understood her sense of responsibility. He couldn't stop thinking about the men at the labor camp who'd tried escaping with him. Men who were hurt or worse. As much as he'd seen these last years, he'd been shocked when one of the men had been shot over and over even after he'd fallen. Quin had been the only one who'd gotten out. He should have tried making it out alone in the first place, should have sent the authorities in to release the rest. That he hadn't done so had been one of the two biggest mistakes in his life.

The other being trusting the woman who'd betrayed him.

He could sense Luz's determination. She wasn't going to give up. With or without him, she was bound to keep going. No one was going to talk her out of searching for her brother. She recognized the danger of what she had to do and it wasn't going to stop her.

He might not trust her, but he respected her for that.

Quin cursed to himself as he recognized the truth: Either he kept Luz Delgado close and protected her, or she would go and get herself killed.

## Chapter Five

Halfway through the night, Luz gave up pretending she was going to sleep. No matter that she was exhausted, it just wasn't happening. Every time she closed her eyes, the horrific day replayed itself in her mind. Trying to block the images—the doctor, the sex acts, her own transformation—was an exercise in futility.

And the nightmare wasn't over. She and Quin weren't home free yet. Wherever they were.

Then again, neither were Diego and Pilar.

What had she been thinking, setting off after her brother alone? If she'd gone to her father and had asked him to hire a private investigator to find Diego, surely he would have done so. Even though he'd never accepted his son into his life, Pappa had always seen to Diego's financial welfare, had even paid for his education. So Pappa must care on some level. What did *she* know about finding people? She was simply the manager of a small bookstore, not a professional.

Not a federal agent like Quin Farrell.

He lay a yard from her, curled on his side toward the still burning embers of the fire, a soft sound whistling through his lips. She wondered how he could sleep so easily.

Maybe because he wasn't afraid.

Throughout their flight, he hadn't shown one sign of the fear that had consumed her. Maybe that was a prerequisite of becoming a lawman—bravery.

She wondered if bravery could be catching.

Moving closer to Quin made her feel better, more settled inside. Safer.

Not many men had done that for her in her life. Certainly no one since Gus. She thought about the young man who'd been a friend of Diego in college. They'd dated for a few months and she'd meant for Gus to be her first. She hadn't loved him the way he had her, but she had cared for him. Before anything serious could happen between them, however, Gus had been killed in a demonstration for Mexican rights they'd marched in—the demonstration had broken into a free-for-all and Gus had died for his ideal.

Luz had been left beaten and bruised, but worse yet, broken-hearted and realizing how fragile life could be.

And how horribly violent.

To her parents' dismay, she'd left school for a job in a nice, safe bookstore. Ever since, she'd lived a quiet life, one that had precluded chancing herself again. One that had allowed her to hide from the world and live in half doses. Nothing had been quiet about the last few days, however. Overnight, she'd been forced awake and her life had been turned upside down.

Luz acknowledged she didn't want to hide anymore, not if it meant losing another person she loved.

Hard to hide dressed as she was. Rather, undressed, she thought, too aware of the skimpy outfit under Quin's shirt. Luz didn't want to be what the brothel's madam and her boss had tried to make of her…yet neither did she want to hide from life the way she'd been doing.

If Quin had his way, that's exactly what he would have her

do, she was certain, but after what she'd been through, Luz wasn't going to stop until she got some answers. She didn't want to live with regret because of unfinished business. She thought Quin understood how important Diego was to her…why she couldn't turn her back on her brother. Staying on this path might be dangerous, but if she did nothing, she wouldn't be able to live with herself.

She could go back to living *safe* later…

Luz looked deep into Quin's face and wondered what it would be like to put one's self in danger for people you didn't even know. Just as Quin had done to get her out of that horrid place. He could have been shot. Or killed.

Quin Farrell was a real-life hero.

With just enough light from the moon to watch him sleep, Luz became fascinated. Despite the beard stubble, he was a good-looking man. His features were rugged, masculine. They suited him. Her gaze went to his cheek and she wondered how he'd gotten that nasty scar.

On the job?

Unable to help herself, she reached out and ran a finger down its length and a thrill shot through her all the way to her toes.

Before she could define the feeling, Quin's eyes shot open and his hand manacled her wrist. Her breath caught in her throat. She couldn't say a word, couldn't look away, couldn't move her hand.

"What are you doing?" he asked.

As she slid in next to him, a sense of anticipation that had been building since she'd met him intensified. "Trying to get closer." As she spoke, her breath mingled with his. "You make me feel safe. I want to thank you."

Groaning softly, Quin let go of her wrist and anchored her head, pulling it to him until his mouth covered hers. Luz's heart began to thud. Even knowing she was entering dangerous territory of a different sort, she parted her lips and let him have his way with her mouth.

It had been eons since she'd kissed a man and she savored every nuance—the tingle of her lips and the catch in her breath and the languorous sensation that spread through her limbs.

Even as she let herself go, let herself rub up against him, Quin broke the kiss and locked gazes with her, as if he were trying to read her mind to determine what it was that she really wanted.

What *did* she want?

Her pulse fluttered through her as she imagined herself locked in a carnal embrace like the ones Maribel had forced her to watch earlier. Only now, instead of being revolted, she was intrigued. Titillated. Tentacles of sweet discomfort spread through her. She'd never meant to be a virgin at this age—it wasn't a matter of morals or beliefs. When Gus had been killed, she'd simply retreated into herself. She'd never wanted to put her emotions on the line like that again.

Remembering Maribel's laughter about her virginity, Luz flushed. Or maybe the heat came directly from contact with Quin.

Quin, who had saved her from a life of forced prostitution or death.

Surely he deserved a reward.

Surely *she* deserved to taste pleasure even if just once, and with a man who meant nothing to her emotionally.

Rationalizing that she had no intention of dying a virgin, Luz slid in closer to Quin. He didn't fight it. He kissed her again, kissed her while somehow undoing the buttons of the shirt she'd taken from his vehicle. In doing so, his fingers skimmed the tops of her breasts, setting them on fire…setting all of her on fire.

Aware of the growing discomfort inside, of the flesh that needed to be appeased, she fumbled with his pants, got them open and released him. Dear Lord, he was bigger than any of the men Maribel had made her watch. Trying not to be intimidated, she copied what she'd seen in that first room—taking his tip in her mouth and slowly sliding her mouth down his shaft.

She was a quick learner.

With a groan, Quin pushed upward and she took him deeper, making heat flare off her every nerve. Throbbing now, she climbed over him. He found her with his fingers.

"You're so wet…and tight," he whispered.

Centering herself over him, Luz took a deep breath and let his tip push through her folds. This was it—the moment she'd been avoiding for far too long.

But before she could sink down his length while controlling the speed and force of the descent, he flipped her over and in one smooth movement pushed himself into her.

The searing pain froze Luz where she lay.

A VIRGIN!

Quin froze.

Dear Lord, she really was a virgin! He'd assumed it had been put on, that the brothel's madam figured he wouldn't know the difference. But apparently he'd been sold the real goods.

Why in the hell hadn't Luz told him this was her first time? Her fear was palpable—it snaked through him and filled all the vacant spaces in his mind until he felt one with her and not just physically.

Quin stared down into Luz's face and wished he could smooth the fright from her expression. There was no going back. The only thing he could do was to replace fear with pleasure.

"It'll be okay," he whispered, moving slowly inside of her.

How could he have known she was innocent—she'd been so aggressive, he'd never stopped to consider the matter. "It'll get better."

But no matter what he tried, no matter how he touched Luz or kissed her, Quin realized that it didn't get better for her. Though she didn't attempt to stop him, neither did she relax beneath him. All her softness was gone. Her features pulled tight as if she were trying to create a mental wall to shut off her feelings, but her fright was too strong. It flayed him and he didn't know how to fix it.

And then it was over.

Release without satisfaction.

Quin rolled to his back and pulled Luz close to his side in an attempt to comfort her. She lay stiffly in his arms.

"I'm only going to hold you, I promise."

He gently stroked her back the way he would a cat. Eventually, her muscles softened and her inner turmoil quieted and her body melted into his.

She was asleep.

Quin tried to relax, but guilt kept him on edge as if he could still feel Luz's distress. He became aware of every little sound from her, every slight change of position. Her face was bathed in moonlight. Her rapid eye movement told him she was dreaming—her features pulled in distress and the smothered sounds she made told him she was having a nightmare.

About what just happened between them?

How was he going to deal with her when she was awake?

Curse his McKenna blood—without it, he wouldn't feel so deeply, wouldn't let guilt weigh him down.

Curse his McKenna blood and the legacy that went with it.

*...dreams are not always tangible things, but more often are born in the heart. Act selflessly in another's behalf, and my legacy shall be yours...*

A legacy that had seemed to make Moira's other grandchildren happy even though they'd gone through hell to find the loves of their lives.

He'd thought he'd found the right woman when he'd met Bianca Ramos a few weeks before his thirty-third birthday, but she'd just turned out to be another curse. Supposedly within thirty-three days of his thirty-third birthday, he was to meet the woman who would make his dreams come true. He'd been taken in by Bianca and she'd turned on him, turned him over to *El Jefe's* men to ensure her own safety. That last part of his grandmother's letter had haunted him from that moment on. He wouldn't make the mistake of trusting the wrong woman again.

Why the hell was he even thinking about his grandmother's legacy now, when for him, it was over?

Luz Delgado had provided him with some relief from the stress they'd shared escaping, that was all. No matter that she vowed to keep searching for her brother, the very idea was ridiculous. She would see that in the light of morning. They would get out of here and back to San Antonio. She would go back to her old life and he would continue on with his mission to end *El Jefe's* reign. They would probably never even see each other again.

That settled, he relaxed and let sleep reclaim him…

"Wake up…c'mon, wake up for me."

A delicate hand fluttered around his face until his eyes opened to a welcome sight—long black hair around beautifully chiseled features and midnight-dark eyes.

*"Bianca, we need some sleep…"*

*But his body had already awakened as it did every time he saw her. So when she slid over him, he didn't fight it.*

*"I need you one last time—"*

"Last?"

"—*before we leave this place,*" *she said.* "*Things will be different tomorrow. I'll be a different person.*"

*Then she was tonguing him, playing with his mouth until he forgot to think and his body simply acted by instinct, his hands capturing her head and holding it steady so he could kiss her as deeply as he took her.*

*When he opened his eyes again, he was on the cot in the cell where he'd been chained. Bianca was there, too, dressed in black leather lingerie and holding a whip, teasing the softness between her thighs with the handle...*

Body covered in sweat, his groin throbbing with the erotic implications of the dream, Quin flew up into a sitting position, only then realizing Luz had still been curled into his side. She landed on her back and half woke.

"Wh-what's going on?"

"Go back to sleep," he said gruffly, trying not to take the dream out on her.

Her eyes fluttered closed and her breasts rose and fell as her breathing deepened. For a moment, he was mesmerized by the fine skin that shone a silver blue in the moonlight. His erection grew more urgent.

Then, hating that he wanted Luz again—blaming the damned dream—he looked away.

Damn! Why did a woman he now hated haunt him like this? He'd had similar dreams before. He'd slept with Bianca that last night before he'd been taken...before she'd turned him in...but the dreams didn't re-create the reality of that night.

None of his dreams were literal—they were another McKenna gift. They tried to tell him something, but it was up to him to figure out what. Things certainly had been different the day after Bianca had betrayed him. She certainly hadn't been the woman he'd thought she was. Nothing new there.

He ran a hand over his face and wondered what he was missing. There was always some deeper truth to his dreams. If he worked on it, surely he would figure it out.

No matter that sleep eluded him the rest of the night, he came to no brilliant conclusions.

What he did come to was the fact that he'd screwed up. Again. What was it with him and bad judgment lately when it came to women? No way on God's earth should he have touched Luz Delgado under the circumstances.

Not that she was another Bianca. He would never again be fooled by a woman.

A glance at a sleeping Luz looking so innocent and vulnerable made something in his stomach curl and he had to fight his inner demons not to react to it, not to wrap himself around her and use his body to keep her safe.

He would be an idiot to follow up on what had been a mindless sex act forged by the danger they'd experienced. There'd been nothing romantic in his deflowering a virgin in the wilderness. And Luz had practically forced herself on him, so there was absolutely no reason for guilt either. None.

With daybreak came some relief even though Luz was having a difficult time looking him in the eyes. With her shapely bare legs on parade and his memory of her lush body that he'd been unable to arouse properly, he was having difficulty looking at her at all.

And so when she announced, "I'm going to clean up at the stream away from camp," Quin should have been relieved, but he wasn't.

As he killed the last embers in the firepit and buried them, he kept thinking about Luz naked, washing body parts he'd touched only hours ago. He tried shaking away the lustful thoughts, but they continued to plague him. He continued to regret what they'd done. What he hadn't been able to do for her, an inner voice added. This wasn't the right place for a woman's first time. He wasn't the right man...

Most of all, she wasn't the right woman. She didn't belong in his dangerous life.

And then Luz returned to camp, muttering, "Lord, I'm starving."

"Is that a request? You want me to go out and kill something—"

"No! Please, don't. I grew up on a ranch and seeing the livestock killed to feed the family and workers put me off meat for a long time. I'm not a vegetarian, but I couldn't eat anything I actually saw die."

Such a romantic, he thought. A couple of days in this wilderness would change her mind. She would eat whatever he could kill raw if she had to.

"What is it you want, then?" he asked. "I doubt there are any edible berries around here."

"I want to get out of here, get back to civilization." Luz looked around, and her voice grew stiff as she asked, "Where are the horses?"

Although Quin didn't see them either, he figured they were nearby. "Don't worry, they're around, just grazing." He whistled for them, using he same repetition of notes he'd used before. "They'll come back."

Thankfully, the horses hadn't wandered off very far. Responding to his call, they picked their way back through the brush as he'd predicted, prancing a bit as if anxious to get back to him.

Quin communicated with them silently, greeting each horse, running his hand up the gelding's forehead and over the poll, then doing the same to the mare, knowing the touch was bonding. He'd always had this connection with animals—and not just horses—ever since he was a kid. Probably the only McKenna gift he actually enjoyed.

Realizing Luz was staring at him—at them—as if she were trying to figure out what was going on, Quin suddenly felt oddly vulnerable.

"We'd better get going," he said, tone gruff. He hadn't let anyone other than family see him work the gift since he was a kid. He'd been considered a freak then, and probably, if he explained things to Luz, she would look at him with that same expression he'd seen on the other kids' faces. "I'll give you a leg up."

Even though she cleared her throat, she didn't say anything but "Right."

Her face was flushed, the color spreading down to her breasts as she positioned herself at the mare's side and slid her foot into his cupped hands. The feel of her smooth skin and warm flesh rocketed through him and knowing she was near-naked under his cotton shirt didn't help. He had to fight himself to stay neutral with her.

He mounted the gelding and took off.

As they rode east toward the sun, he checked for a cell signal every five minutes. A half hour out, in the midst of a huge clearing away from canyon walls, he finally scared up a couple of bars and immediately stopped his horse before he lost it again.

"Eureka!" he growled, his gaze meeting Luz's.

Her eyes flashed closed as if she were giving silent thanks, yet her spine stiffened as if she couldn't quite believe her ordeal was over and she was bracing herself for further disappointment. Wanting to reassure her, he knew only one way. He pulled up Aaron's cell number and hit Send. Seconds later, his buddy answered.

"Quin, where the hell are you?"

"I was hoping you could tell me that. And then send someone to come get us."

Quin gave him an abbreviated explanation of what had

happened while Aaron triangulated their location via the cell phone GPS.

"Got it!" Aaron said. "Stay put so you keep that signal. I'll send a helicopter out straight away to pick you up."

Straight away could mean anything from a half hour to half a day, Quin thought, depending on whether or not someone insisted Aaron do paperwork before anything was done.

Anxious to get Luz back to civilization, Quin said, "We're going to keep heading the horses east, Aaron. Staying put could get us killed."

"You think they're still after you?"

"What do you think?" A rhetorical question. Quin didn't wait for an answer. "While you're at it," he said, looking directly at Luz, "send in a team to close down the brothel and make some arrests."

"Will do."

As he flipped the cell closed, Luz softened as did her expression. "It's really over then?"

"Almost," Quin said, despite the fact that the back of his neck was suddenly feeling itchy, like someone was on his trail. "Let's keep moving straight east."

"All right."

Quin concentrated and made a mental connection with the horses and got them going again in the right direction.

Seeming a bit more light-hearted, Luz urged her mare into a lope, his shirt-tails blowing up her back. Quin enjoyed the scenery for a moment before squeezing his gelding's sides to follow.

The expanse ahead seemed endless. A half hour passed… then another…and still they weren't out of the bowels of the canyon. A while more and they were zigzagging up the switchback trail to the flat above when Quin caught a faint thwack-thwack coming from somewhere ahead.

"Did you hear that?" A flushed Luz threw a glance over her shoulder toward him.

Quin drew his mount alongside hers. "That would be a helicopter—our ride home is headed this way."

"What about the horses?"

"We'll just let them go. Chances are they'll find their way back to their pasture. That is, if the guards from the brothel don't round them up first."

The statement made Luz throw a nervous look over her shoulder. Quin gave the area behind them a good look, too, but saw nothing untoward.

As they took the last turn of the switchback, the sound of the chopper receded. Then it seemed to circle as if the pilot was looking for them. Quin tightened his thighs and the gelding sped up, Luz's mare sticking right behind him.

As they rose to the flat above the canyon, he was looking up into the sky to get a bead on the aircraft. When he spotted the chopper, he waved both arms to get the pilot's attention.

Until a sharp sound and dirt churning up in front of him alerted Quin to trouble.

Two men on horses broke out of a stand of trees and a black truck followed. Both mounted men bore guns—one a rifle. The rifleman stood in his saddle and took aim at them.

And Quin communicated the need for flight to the horses.

# Chapter Six

The mare took off. Luz squealed in surprise and hung on with all her might. It took her a moment to realize that someone was shooting at them from behind. Her pulse thundered through her and her stomach knotted.

Where was the damn helicopter? She could hear it but couldn't see it.

In front of her, Quin gestured wildly, urging her to go faster. Not knowing if it was possible, she dug her heels into the mare's sides, and seeing jagged rock scattered before them, prayed they would make it to the clearing ahead without breaking their necks.

Then suddenly the helicopter appeared, looking like it slid out of a hill of rocks and trees. It hovered in the distance over the clearing. Boulders strewn along the path prevented it from landing closer.

Another bullet whined by her, smashing into rock. She flattened herself over the mare's neck and glanced back only to see the distance between them and the men chasing them was closing.

"Get ahead of me!" Quin yelled, slowing a bit so she pulled alongside him.

"What are you doing?"

"Go! Go! Go!"

Luz barely squeezed her legs and the mare jumped and shot ahead, racing hell-bent-for-leather. Her heart raced, too, as fast as the mare's legs pumped. Fear tore through her, not for herself, but for the man who was putting himself between her and the line of fire!

If something happened to him because of her...

A blanket of dust rose from the ground as the helicopter hovered a few feet above land, barely a hundred yards away. They were almost there, but would they both make it?

Glancing back, she saw Quin's body jerk. Dear God, was he hit! How bad? If he died, she would be to blame! Wishing she had reins to turn the mare back in that direction, Luz sent up a quick prayer and strained to see Quin—he leaned slightly to one side, but he kept his seat.

Gunfire was being returned from the opposite direction. She looked to the helicopter. A uniformed man with a high-powered rifle was standing on one of the skids.

The men pursuing them immediately gave way and headed for cover.

"Keep your head down!" Quin shouted.

*Shouted...*

Then he couldn't be injured too seriously. Her roiling stomach steadied.

A thankful Luz did as he said and slowed her mount as they neared the chopper's whirling blades. The mare spooked anyway and tried breaking away from the raucous noise, from the threat of the whirling blades, but Quin pulled the gelding alongside and cut her off from making a run for it.

"Dismount now!"

Luz didn't wait for him to tell her again. She slid off the mare, who whirled and nearly flew away from the rotors. Quin followed, grabbed her around the waist and practically carried her through a cloud of dust to the helicopter's door where the uniformed man pulled her on board. Seconds later, Quin was sitting next to her and the helicopter was quickly rising.

The noise was so loud she had to cover her ears with both hands. The guy in the uniform handed her headgear that muffled the piercing sound. Then she looked to Quin, who leaned back against the seat, seeming drained of energy and most of the color in his face. He was cradling his left arm, his sleeve smeared with his blood.

Knowing he was hurt because of her, Luz's chest tightened. "How bad is it? Can I do anything?" she yelled, but she couldn't even hear herself, so how could he.

Apparently he understood, though, for his forehead pulled tight and he shook his head. The uniformed guy opened some kind of kit and pulled out a tourniquet that he wrapped around Quin's arm above the hit.

He would be all right, she told herself, suddenly thinking of the way he'd cradled her against him after she'd forced her virginity on him. Just thinking about it made her warm through-and-through. Embarrassment, she told herself, that was all. She was simply embarrassed that she'd made a fool of herself. If Quin thought so, though, she couldn't tell. He'd treated her with decency. He might not have been her dream lover, but he was decent. Not to mention he was the best damn protector she could ever want.

Certain Quin wouldn't have been wounded at all if he hadn't tried to save her, Luz wondered what she could ever do to repay him.

AN AMBULANCE was waiting for them when they touched down at Lackland Air Force Base a short while later. Medics hauled a stretcher to the cabin door as Quin stepped down to the tarmac.

He tried waving the medics away. "I don't need any stretcher."

"You're bleeding and you need to be checked out," one of the medics argued.

"I *was* bleeding—"

"What's wrong with you?" Luz yelled. "You were shot!"

"It's a flesh wound!" he shouted back even as the engines were cut and they could speak normally again.

Her face flushed, Luz grabbed his good arm like she wasn't about to let go and seemed determined to drag him toward the ambulance. "You're going to let them check out that wound and clean it, and if they say you need to go to the hospital, you're going."

Quin sensed the reason for her concern. "You're not to blame."

"Who said I was?"

Her emotions did, only she didn't know that he knew it. Not wanting to press the issue, he did the sensible thing and went with her voluntarily.

"I sure would like to know how the hell we could be so unlucky for them to find us before we could get on the copter," he grumbled.

Twenty minutes later, the wound was inspected, cleaned, disinfected and bandaged. The bleeding had stopped on its own and he hadn't had enough loss to put him at risk.

He slid out of the back of the ambulance, saying, "Good as new."

"Not exactly."

Waves of her uncertainty surrounded him, but before he could reassure her, a car pulled up and Aaron got out.

"What are you doing here?" Quin asked, surprised that Aaron had come in person.

"Making sure you're still alive and bringing you back to the SAC office."

"What about the raid on the brothel?"

Aaron shook his head. "Too late. Must've fled the scene when they didn't get you yesterday. Let's get going. You need to be debriefed." He turned from Quin to Luz. "You, too."

"Like this?" She looked down to her bare legs and feet. "Can we stop at my place first so I can get cleaned up and put on some real clothes?"

Quin kind of liked her disheveled appearance, bare legs and all.

"We could go to your place first," Aaron said, "if you promise not to call anyone until we get your story."

"But my parents might be concerned not having heard from me in days..." Luz sighed but nodded in agreement and gave Aaron her address in the historic Monte Vista neighborhood.

Twenty minutes later, they pulled up to a large courtyard apartment building.

"I'll be quick."

"I'm coming inside with you," Quin said. "Just in case."

A flicker of fear crossed her features, but she quickly hid it. She couldn't hide feelings, though. He sensed hesitation. And embarrassment, undoubtedly at the way she was dressed. Rather, undressed.

"Don't worry," he said as they crossed the tiled courtyard. "There's no one around to see you."

"How did you know what I was thinking?"

He lifted an eyebrow. "I read your mind."

"Yeah, right."

Laughing nervously, she took tiled stairs to a second-floor apartment with a private balcony overlooking the fountain, pool and gazebo.

When she stopped at the entrance, he asked, "How do you plan on getting in?"

"With a key, of course."

She indicated a pot with a nasty-looking cactus, then, rather than lifting it to get that key, surprised him by poking a finger into the dirt and squirreling it out. At least that was original—he'd expected the key to be under the planter. Undoubtedly the cactus would prevent someone from messing with it anyway.

After using his shirt to wipe down the key, she unlocked the front door.

"Let me go in first," Quin insisted.

"That's not necessary." She started to enter but he grabbed her upper arm and stopped her. Trying to wrench her arm free, she asked, "What are you doing?"

"Trying to keep you from getting yourself in more trouble."

She stopped fighting him and he went inside, checked the place over in thirty seconds and then let her in.

"I won't be long," she promised, heading for the bedroom.

"I can wait."

And discover a bit more about her while he did.

He needed to take his mind off the sounds of her moving around, of the shower running…

The apartment was big, he thought—two bedrooms, bath and a half, with a dining nook off the kitchen rather than a formal dining room. The floors were hardwood in the living areas, colorful ceramic tile in the kitchen and baths, all decorated with area rugs that looked perfect for each space, as if she'd spent a lot of time finding each one. Her attention to detail was evident in her choice of color on the walls and couch, in the artwork and plants and the books filling the shelves on either side of the tiled fireplace. He'd seen another bookcase in her bedroom and an entire wall of books in the spare.

The apartment wasn't small, but it was warm and cozy, Quin thought, unable to stop remembering moments of their time together. They played through his head like a photo album and he couldn't seem to make them stop. Like the occupant, Luz's apartment was very inviting.

And totally the opposite of his place. After moving in, he'd never even unpacked all his boxes.

Quin threw himself in a leather chair with a decorative hand-tooled back, and before he knew it, had a black and white cat in his lap. She was purring like a little motorboat before he even touched her. Touch her he did—long, soothing strokes along her spine and tail.

Which reminded him of the way he'd stroked Luz after they'd had sex. She'd shown a vulnerability then, something she'd been quick to hide come morning. He wasn't certain which side of her he preferred.

"So where have you been hiding?" he asked the cat and immediately got a vague impression of a pile of clothes in a dark space and feminine hands reaching in toward the cat. "I wonder what secrets you could tell me about your mistress."

"Do you really think Blossom would dish on the woman who feeds her?"

At the sound of Luz's voice, the cat jumped out of his lap and whirled around Luz's legs, now covered by beige trousers, which were topped by a sea-green shirt. She'd pulled her wet hair up and clipped it in back and had donned silver and green turquoise earrings and a big chunky bracelet to match.

"You clean up fast."

He was actually thinking about how good she looked… how tempting…

"One more minute to open a can of tuna for Blossom. She's been eating nothing but crunchies from her feeder since I've been gone."

Relieved that he had a minute to gather himself together— reacting to her physically wasn't an indulgence he could justify—Quin was waiting for her in the open doorway when she came back from the kitchen.

"I brought this," she said, indicating the shoulder bag, "but there's not much in it. The men who grabbed me must have my cell phone and wallet, which means they got my driver's license, birth certificate, one of my credit cards and my ATM card. I didn't even think about all that until now. And then there's my SUV."

"When we get to the office, I'll have staff help expedite replacements for the cards and birth certificate." Luckily she didn't yet need a passport to cross the border—that would take time to replace. "And we can get someone in Nuevo Laredo to check on your vehicle until I can arrange a pickup."

"If it's still there."

Finding out was the first thing he did when they arrived at the SAC office. While Aaron went to start the paperwork on the case, Quin called the customs and immigration checkpoint and asked them to send one of the workers to check. Twenty minutes later, he got his answer.

The vehicle was gone.

When he told Luz, she took it in stride, while he wondered what to make of it. Probably it had simply been stolen off the street by some lowlife looking for a fancy ride. Or looking to sell it for drug money.

But what if that hadn't been the case? What if *El Jefe's* people had known all along who Luz was—that Diego was her brother? What if they wanted her back badly enough to pick her up here in San Antonio?

Quin didn't voice the thought. No use in scaring Luz to death.

"What now?" she asked.

"Now Aaron will debrief you and I have to report to my SAC."

"SAC?"

"The Special Agent in Charge of this office." Thinking about her missing vehicle and the implications that worried him, he said, "You have family here in San Antonio, right?"

"My parents have a ranch a short ride from the city."

"I suggest when your debriefing is over, you let us escort you there. After what you've been through, you could use some R&R."

"I don't need R&R," she said.

"You also don't need to be alone for a while."

"I want to find my brother."

"He'll be on our radar—"

"Not good enough!"

Even though Quin felt her gearing up for an all-out fight, he said, "You need to tend to your own life and let me tend to my investigation."

Indignation coloring her face, Luz shot to her feet. "Your saving me from that hellhole doesn't make you the boss of me, Quin Farrell. You do what you need to do and I'll do the same. I'll find Diego without your help." She looked around wildly as if for an escape route.

Realizing she wasn't going to give up, Quin grasped her arm before she could move. He couldn't let her take that kind of risk. The next time she might end up dead.

"All right, I get it," he said. "You want to help. Fine. But *I* run this operation. You defer to me. To make it clear, that *does* mean I'm the boss of you."

Her face flushed with color and for a moment she didn't speak, but her anger and frustration washed over him. In the end she pulled herself together and nodded curtly.

"All right. I'm in. You're the boss. We'll do things your way."

Quin gave her a satisfied grin. Pulling her arm free, she flipped around and headed for the interrogation room where Aaron was waiting for her.

Which left him to face SAC Maria Gonzales alone.

He found her filing paperwork in her office. She looked up at him over her reading glasses and indicated he should take

a seat. Then she went back to her document and let him wait.
And wait. One of Maria's specialties was knowing exactly
how long to make a person sweat.

Indeed, Quin found himself starting to squirm in his seat
before she looked up again.

Maria removed her glasses and lay them on the desk before
her. "What do you have to say for yourself?"

That was certainly direct, Quin thought, saying, "That I
rescued a U.S. citizen who'd been human trafficked to one of
*El Jefe's* brothels."

"You weren't on active duty."

"Should I have ignored the situation? Let Luz Delgado be
used by who knows how many men—"

"You didn't come upon that situation by accident, Quin.
You ignored orders and deliberately continued your investigation alone."

"Nevertheless, we now have someone willing to testify
against *El Jefe* when we get his ass!"

"Are you certain of that?" Maria asked. "Did Ms. Delgado
see *El Jefe*? Hear him called by name?"

"She might have seen him. The point is—"

"The point is you acted recklessly, Quin. As a Special
Agent, your obsessive behavior is unacceptable."

"Are you going to fire me?"

Her anger flared a notch, but it didn't show other than in
the brightness of her eyes as she glared at him. "You're one
of my best. I would rather come to terms with you."

"Then know this. I can't let it go."

"I wasn't asking you to let it go but to wait until you're
cleared for duty and then to work as part of a team."

"When will that happen?"

"Considering the new circumstances, it might be longer
than you like."

Quin got to his feet. "Then I'm taking vacation time, effective immediately."

"Quin, sit back down!" Maria stared at him, hard-faced but silent, until he did. "Don't be a fool. You've already been shot. I don't want to see you hurt further…maybe killed."

"Thanks for the faith in me."

"I do have faith in you, but you're only one man. You can't bring down *El Jefe's* entire operation alone!"

Quin shrugged. "Who said I was going to try?"

Maria wasn't buying the innocent act. Shaking her head, she said, "Then what is it you think you can do? Some men learn from their mistakes."

"I've learned a lot, Maria, starting with the fact that I'm not the forgiving type. I want to break *El Jefe's* operation and put him behind bars forever. I'm not delusional. I know I can't do it alone. But with my personal stake in the investigation, I'm motivated to get to the truth. And I'm not waiting for any shrink's go-ahead. I'm serious about that vacation time."

"All right, you have it." Maria rubbed her hand over her eyes. "I can't sanction putting you back on active duty before Dr. Avila clears you. And I know I can't stop you from doing what you feel you must, but please don't put yourself at risk. If you get anything we can use, I want you to come to me before you act."

Knowing his doing so would be unlikely, he nevertheless said, "I'll keep that in mind."

# Chapter Seven

The moment Quin walked in the door of his apartment, he headed for the bedroom. Washed through with exhaustion, he nevertheless saw the inadequacy of the way he lived compared to Luz. The walls were as white as the day he'd moved in with intentions of painting. Unpacked boxes lined the area under the windows. The few pieces of furniture he owned—couch, chair, a couple of tables—were all of decent design, but they simply looked as if they were sitting in some warehouse rather than in someone's home.

Entering the bedroom with its king-sized bed and mule dresser, he felt the same way. Still, the nondecor was good enough for a much-needed sleep. He threw himself on the bed, closed his eyes and let his mind drift.

It drifted straight to Luz Delgado the way she'd looked when he'd first seen her. One look at her had been enough to give any man a hard-on, and yet he'd liked her better without all the artifice.

He could hear Luz begging him to help her again and he wondered how many innocent women pulled from their homes to be sold like cattle had begged only to be ignored.

It had to stop and he had to stop it. He wouldn't rest until *El Jefe's* operation was closed down and he was behind bars.

Or dead.

He'd been thinking a lot about that lately—dead was a sure way he wouldn't walk on some technicality or deal. The question was—could he really do it?

Quin pulled a hand over his face.

What had happened to him?

When had he changed?

He used to have standards. He used to see things in black or white, right or wrong. He used to recognize there were lines that couldn't be crossed.

He guessed he still did—he just didn't have the same respect for those lines as he once had, not when it seemed the evil involved had more power than the law.

The evil made him sick and if he couldn't stop it, what good was he?

Again, he heard the desperation in Luz's voice when she'd begged him to help her escape.

Thank God he'd been able to do so.

Now he just had to keep her out of harm's way while running his private investigation. If he wasn't certain she would act without him, he would leave her behind and never look back. That she might be able to get him some leads he couldn't get himself was in her favor.

He closed his eyes again and tried harder to sleep, but every time he started to float off, Luz was there waiting for him in all her incarnations—whore, angel, avenger.

She'd gotten under his skin and he didn't need another woman that close, breathing down his neck, betraying him if that was most convenient for her. Not after what he'd gone through because of Bianca. Refusing to dream of the woman again, as he surely would if he fell asleep, Quin got out of bed, putting sleep on hold for a while longer.

Perhaps it wasn't fair to distrust Luz, but he didn't trust

himself. He still didn't understand what had happened to cloud his judgment so badly that he'd ended up a victim in his own case.

It had to be the McKenna legacy, which went beyond the gifts he and his siblings and first cousins had inherited from their grandmother.

The top left drawer of the mule dresser was reserved for important paperwork, including the letter. Fetching it, he unfolded the worn missive. He'd read it so many times that the folds threatened to rip. He held it carefully—the only tangible thing he had of his grandmother—and read.

*To my darling grandchildren,*

*I leave you my love and more. Within thirty-three days after your thirty-third birthday—enough time to know what you are about—you will have in your grasp a legacy of which your dreams are made. Dreams are not always tangible things, but more often are born in the heart. Act selflessly in another's behalf, and my legacy shall be yours.*

*Your loving grandmother,*

*Moira McKenna*

*PS    Use any other inheritance from me wisely and only for good lest you destroy yourself or those you love.*

It had all fallen into place for him. Or so he'd thought. He'd been trying to act selflessly in another's behalf and the thirty-third birthday timing had been perfect. Too bad Bianca hadn't been.

Too bad he hadn't met Luz…

What the hell was he thinking?

He folded up his grandmother's letter and put it away. Luz Delgado wasn't the woman for him. Perhaps no woman was.

His life was too dangerous. If any woman with heart and conviction took a chance on him, he'd probably get her killed.

So why had the legacy come true for his siblings and his cousins? He was the youngest, the last to turn thirty-three, probably the only one still alone. Or *had* it come true for all of his cousins? Quin wondered. He'd been out of touch with family so long—it had been a few years, this time—he didn't know.

Something made him want to find out.

He did the thing he swore he would never do until this case was closed—he called home. Rather, he called his sister, Kate, in South Dakota.

When she recognized his voice, she squealed. "Quin! Thank God you're all right!"

"I'm fine." All but for the twinge in his arm that reminded him he could have been killed that morning if the rifleman had been a better shot. "I want to know about all of you. How are Mom and Dad? And Neil and you?"

"We're all good…not that you care enough to let us know where you are or how to reach you! Where the hell have you been?"

"Here and there," he said, trying to remain vague despite her frustration.

"Well, while you were incommunicado, you became an uncle twice over. Neil and Annabeth's son Jeremy is nearly two. And Chase's and my Maggie will be six months old next week. She can't talk yet, of course, but she chatters in her own language. I call her Magpie. You know, after the crows we used to listen to when we were kids."

He'd wondered if he was an uncle and now he knew. Warmth unfurled inside him. And a longing he didn't want to look at too closely. It didn't do to want what he couldn't have.

"Congratulations to you both, Katydid," he said picking up the kid nickname like he'd used it yesterday.

Nostalgia for home and family wrapped its powerful tentacles around his heart and for a moment Quin wished he could step back in time and make different decisions about how he was going to live his life. For a moment he wished he'd agreed to work the ranch with his brother, Neil, wished he'd found a nice girl to marry and have half a dozen kids.

But of course, that wasn't the legacy.

"You should be here, Quin," Kate said, suddenly sounding weepy. "At least some of the time. Every time you disappear, we worry about you. We make up stories about what you're doing to make ourselves feel better. Mom and Dad have convinced themselves you're on exciting adventures hunting treasure in remote places like you always said you wanted to when we were kids. Neil thinks you're in some kind of trouble with the law. I'd rather think you're an undercover agent."

She fell silent as if she were waiting for confirmation or denial. Quin clenched his jaw. He knew he should tell his sister something—anything—but he just couldn't. He'd always kept his past and present separate—initially out of necessity and now because he didn't want his loved ones to be tainted by what he did.

By what he *might* do.

He finally said, "You and Neil always did have wild imaginations."

"So you're a treasure hunter?"

"I'm no Indiana Jones," he said.

"Keelin dreamed you were in trouble, Quin. She saw terrible things…things she said you were seeing…men being beaten and shot…"

Keelin was the McKenna cousin who'd been closest to their Grandmother Moira. She'd inherited the dream ability of seeing through another's eyes—knowing what really was happening rather than having to guess as he did—especially if the other person was in trouble. Keelin must have tuned into his prison break the other night.

"It was just a dream," he lied. "Tell her I'm fine." He paused a moment before asking, "What about the legacy? Aileen and Flanna—?"

"Both found their mates," Kate said before he could even finish asking the question. "It's your turn to find your soul mate, Quin. Unless you've already found her. Is that why you're really calling?"

His chest tightened. "Afraid not, Katydid."

No way would he ever tell his sister about Bianca and what had happened to him. No way would he share his guilt at what had happened to the men in that labor camp. No way would he make his family privy to his work—not the way he felt about it now.

"I don't understand. You were thirty-three last month. You should have at least met her by now."

The reason he'd believed Bianca was the one. He'd been seduced by her, had fallen for her lies and the emotions he'd read off her. But he'd never felt real love for her. Yet, since he'd turned thirty-three, he had assumed—had convinced himself—that she had to be the one.

"I guess I'm the exception to the legacy."

Luz suddenly came to mind, but Quin wiped it away. It was too late for him. He accepted that. He ended the conversation with his sister, telling Kate he needed to get back to work.

Another lie.

He turned off the cell that issued no call-back number and wondered how long he could go on like this, separated from his family, on some damn mission that usually brought him more crap than commendations.

One more, he thought. He would close down *El Jefe* and then he would reconsider his life.

HER GRUELING DEBRIEFING over, Luz let Aaron drop her off at her apartment. Quin had promised to call her first thing in the morning, so she'd picked up another cell phone on the way. Both her credit card company and bank would express replacements by the next morning. Quin had promised he would expedite copies of her driver's license and birth certificate, too.

Once she got inside, she would call the owner of the bookstore, tell him that she needed to take some vacation time immediately. That is, if he didn't fire her for going missing the last few days.

Exhausted, she wanted nothing more than a good night's sleep in her own bed. To deal with Quin Farrell, she needed to be on her A-game in the morning.

What had she been thinking, giving up her virginity to him? She'd wanted the passing to be special, something to remember always. She guessed she would remember, if not in a particularly positive way. She would always associate that first time with violence, even though she'd instigated the act herself.

Truthfully, in the end, it was the association with violence that had frozen her, had made it impossible for her to relax and enjoy what Quin had to offer.

About to unlock her front door, Luz realized it was already open a crack. Her heart pounded and she backed off, wildly wondering what to do now.

The conservative part of her told her to turn tail and run as fast as she could and only when she was someplace safe would she call the authorities about a break-in.

Too bad she didn't listen.

Too bad she had to know who was inside.

Her pulse threading unevenly, Luz was reaching for the door when it swung open, the unexpected action throwing her back against the railing.

"Lucy! Where have you been?" her father demanded, his

short silver hair practically bristling. "Your mother is sick to death with worry."

Dominick Delgado appeared worried as well. His forehead was pulled, making his dark eyes look even deeper set. He had only a few inches on Luz, but he stood straight-spined, which made him seem larger than life somehow.

"Pappa." She took a deep breath and felt her pulse steady, then pulled herself together. "How good to see you." Moving to him, she brushed his cheek with her lips, tickled as she always was by his full mustache.

"That's not an answer."

"And I'm not a child to be questioned."

"You're *my* child, Lucy."

He still called her by the nickname he considered more American than Luz, even though she'd been Luz to everyone else for several years.

"So is Diego."

"What does Diego have to do with this?"

"He's missing, Pappa. I haven't heard from him for a week now and I'm sick with worry."

"He probably went on vacation and just didn't tell you."

"No, Pappa, this is serious. His girlfriend, Pilar, disappeared and he was trying to find her. And then he disappeared. No one has heard from Diego. For all we know, he was taken off the street like a stray dog."

"But *you*…where have you been?"

She thought to tell her father the truth of what had happened to her, but she feared he would lock her up himself to protect her. Besides, she simply couldn't worry her parents like that.

"I've been to Diego's apartment among other things."

"You crossed the border?"

Knowing how he felt—that she should ignore her heritage,

which included staying out of Mexico—Luz didn't answer, merely shouldered by him to get inside. He could see she was all right, and yet all his concern seemed to be over her rather than for his missing son.

"I don't understand, Pappa," she said, a catch in her voice, "I always thought you were so caring. How could you be so cold about your own son?"

"I'm concerned for him, of course, but you—"

"You're *concerned* for Diego? I never noticed."

"I did my duty by him."

"Duty? You think supporting him financially is enough?" Luz had never spoken this way to her father before. "What about Diego's emotional welfare? What about his heart? His mother is dead, Pappa. We're all he has."

"What do you expect me to do?"

"Welcome him into the family. *If* he's still alive."

At dusk, they set him on horseback, his hands tied behind him, duct tape covering his mouth. Diego wanted to demand to know what they would do with him now, wanted to know what they'd done with Pilar, but trying to talk with his mouth taped was futile. He needed all his energy—when he saw his chance, he would somehow make a run for it.

One of his two captors and the apparent leader checked the girth of his own saddle, then looked over to a third man who was inspecting a high-powered rifle with a scope.

"Now it's time for some fun!" the leader told him.

"That's what I'm counting on."

The other captor spoke up. "But he has only five minutes on us."

"That's enough," the leader said. "We don't wanna raise his hopes too high."

"Not enough time for him to get anywhere near the river."

"Maybe there won't be enough left of him to worry about it," the leader said. "Go take care of the cat."

Grumbling, the one following orders threw himself into his saddle and rode off without them.

The cat?

He was sure they didn't mean a house cat. He'd heard what sounded like the roar of a mountain lion the last few nights, but he'd thought one of the rarely seen cats had just wandered in too close to the buildings.

The guy who'd kept his distance put his rifle in a leather sheath attached to the saddle and mounted his horse.

Diego watched the leader swing into the saddle and grab the reins. Although he braced himself, when the man clucked and both mounts moved forward, he jerked back hard and had to fight to stay upright.

Questions roiled through his mind the way acid roiled through his stomach as they rode west toward the river, through a tangle of mesquites and black brush. His mind floated off for a moment, as he thought of the woman he loved. Suddenly, he was brought back to his own situation as he caught a cloud of dust and movement ahead—a man was running away from them as if his very life depended on it.

And then he realized it did. He understood what this was about. He'd heard even back in Mexico, but he hadn't wanted to believe.

The leader snickered. "See that guy? He thinks he's getting away from us. Going home."

"Well, he might be going home," the third man said, "but it's not to Mexico."

The leader snickered some more and stopped the horses. "Here's your shot. Do it."

The runner threw a panicked look over his shoulder. Poor guy was terrified and had a right to be—he was the prey in the ultimate hunt. Indeed, there *were* worse things than being enslaved into forced labor and prostitution.

The third man pulled the rifle from his saddle and took aim. Even so, he didn't take the shot right away. His muscles tensed and a rivulet of sweat rolled down his forehead. He seemed unsure…

"Do it now!" the leader ordered.

A single shot whipped the runner's head back but he kept going.

Horrified, Diego watched as the man aimed again.

A second shot and the runner stumbled to his knees. His shirt bloomed red high on the shoulder on one side, low on the waist on the other, but the wounded man somehow got back to his feet and forced his legs to work. Lurching forward, he looked like a broken puppet.

The man with the rifle cursed and aimed again, but before he could take his shot, a low roar broke the silence. Seemingly out of nowhere came a whirl of motion—two hundred pounds of pissed-off mountain lion leaping nearly twenty feet from the rocks to land directly on him.

The *prey* went down for a final time.

Swallowing bile, Diego looked away, but the leader backed up his horse and forced his head around.

"Watch!" his captor demanded as the big cat tore into the poor man. "Unless you talk, tell us everything we want to know, that'll be you!"

# Chapter Eight

Luz's stomach knotted as they left customs and immigration and drove into Nuevo Laredo. She'd cleared the time off with her boss—thankfully, she'd have a job to go back to when this was over.

The first thing she and Quin did when they got into town was to make out a stolen vehicle report. And then they headed for Diego's apartment building.

Quin parked his pickup truck not so far from where her SUV had been stolen. Paranoid now, Luz glanced all around her to see if anyone was watching them. She didn't see anyone, but as she'd learned the last time, that didn't mean anything. Thankfully, she was with a man who could take care of whatever or whoever came up.

She didn't want to ruminate any longer on her foolishness at having sex with Quin. A big disappointment and now a seeming sticking point between them. She couldn't help but be drawn to such a powerful man. At the same time, she felt a little weird around him and suspected Quin felt the same, and here they were, reluctant partners due to their common goal.

*What a mistake…*

"You okay?"

Terrified, Luz took a deep breath. "Yeah, sure. Let's do it."

Doing it meant facing building owner Jacinta Herrera.

Luz stayed close to Quin's side until they entered Nuevo Laredo Artesania.

Jacinta's surprise at seeing Luz quickly faded away.

Still, Luz hadn't missed it. "Surprised to see me?"

No answer.

"Where can we talk in private?"

"My customers—"

"Can wait," Quin finished for her. "You can talk to us or you can talk to the *Federales*."

The woman stiffened, and for a moment, Luz didn't think she would do it. Then Jacinta nodded and asked her assistant to take over for her. She led them to her private quarters at the back of the store.

Sunlight streamed through tall windows across the saltillo tiled floor and the hand-carved and painted furniture—table and chairs, a bench near the windows, a trunk tucked in a corner. As Luz might have expected, the living area was filled with the kind of area rugs and artwork found in the shop.

One wall merely had two portraits of women…and ceramic masks of their faces. Luz remembered Jacinta's niece and her daughter were missing, too.

"Why are you here?" the shop owner asked.

"Why…or how?" Luz returned. Jacinta surely knew. "When I left my brother's apartment, I was taken and drugged and trafficked back into Texas where they put me in a brothel."

"Oh, *Dios mio*, I feared it was something like that." The woman crumbled before Luz's eyes. She sank into an upholstered chair and moaned.

"Feared?" Luz asked.

"I thought I heard something and came around to see a man getting into the back seat of a black Lincoln before it took off.

That is all. I swear I did not even think you might be inside until later."

Even so, Luz read the guilt in Jacinta's expression.

"If you *had* known," Quin said, "what would you have done? Alerted the authorities?"

Jacinta waited a breath too long before saying, "Yes, of course."

"I thought you felt they wouldn't do anything," Luz said.

"Then I would have contacted your people."

Quin shook his head in disbelief. "Sounds like you're making it up as you go along."

"You cannot think I had anything to do your being taken from here."

Ignoring the masks on the wall that seemed to be staring at her, Luz asked, "Why shouldn't I?"

"Because, I am on the other side!"

"Other side of what?" Suddenly it came to Luz—she stared directly at the masks of the missing women related to the shop owner. "Jacinta, are you some part of a vigilante group that's trying to find the missing victims?"

"What?" Quin's tone and expression intensified before he turned his gaze to the masks, then back to the shop owner. He stared at Jacinta as if he was trying to read her mind. "If it's true, we need to know everything."

Still, the shop owner wasn't talking. But Luz could see she was weakening. Her eyes were watery and she was picking at the material of her long skirt. Luz moved to her, crouched before her and took the woman's hands in her own.

"Why didn't you tell me the other day when I came to find my brother?"

"Diego wouldn't have wanted you involved with *La Liberación Humana*."

Human liberation…so there was more of a reason for the

masks in the shop than Jacinta's relatives, Luz thought. They signified a movement to retrieve those who were trafficked.

"You don't know that Diego wouldn't have wanted us to know about…" Luz let her voice fade. "Or do you? Was Diego a member of the group?"

Jacinta nodded. "His woman, too. Her cousin went missing several months ago. Pilar found someone who could give her information and made an appointment to talk to him. She called to say she'd recorded his statement about what he'd seen. And then she never returned."

Luz could hardly believe Diego never told her the whole truth. Why had he kept his involvement in trying to rescue trafficking victims to himself? She got to her feet and went to the wall with the masks. She stared at the ceramics as if they, too, held secrets.

Quin asked, "You think *El Jefe's* men learned what Pilar had done that fast and then removed her?"

Jacinta's eyes were sad. "I am afraid so."

"Do you know the name of this witness?"

"Juan de los Reyes."

"Where can we find him?"

"In the cemetery. He had a fatal accident the day after he talked to Pilar. A car ran him down in the street."

Luz gasped and whirled to face them. "You're saying they killed him to shut him up?"

"We're not dealing with Boy Scouts, Luz!" Quin snapped. "I thought you got that by now."

"Not Boy Scouts…but *killers?*"

Luz didn't know why that shocked her after what she'd been through. Quin was certainly no Boy Scout himself. To tell the truth, the long hair and beard stubble and the aggressive stance he took at every turn reminded her more of a street criminal than a crime fighter. So why did he continue to have the power to make her breathless when he moved too close? Why couldn't she forget what happened between them out in the wilderness? Why did she wonder what it would be like if they tried again?

Snapping herself back to the issue, she asked Jacinta, "What about Diego? What haven't you told me about what happened to him?"

How much more did the woman know?

"Nothing, I swear." The shop owner fell silent for a moment, then said, "Something made me check his apartment the night you showed up. Someone had been in there—possibly the people who took you. Diego's computer was gone and the place was a mess, like they'd been trying to find something."

"Were they looking for an object?" Quin asked. "Or for information?" When Luz gave him a questioning look, he said, "The computer. Maybe someone wanted to look over the contents at his leisure."

Luz felt a stress headache coming on. She wished in the worst way that she was back in her nice, safe bookshop. "This is getting more complicated by the minute."

"Just before Diego went after Pilar," Jacinta said, "he told me that those people ending up in enforced labor or prostitution were the lucky ones. I do not know with whom he had spoken, but there was this new pall about him as if he had information that was somehow unbearable. He said there were worse things that could happen to a person…"

"My God, what?"

The woman shook her head. "I do not know. I do not think I want to know."

"Is there anyone who *does* know?" Quin asked.

"Maybe. What he said made me think Pilar learned something important. She had told me she was going to record the conversation with the witness. Maybe someone else heard it."

"*After* she disappeared," Quin said.

Jacinta shrugged. "Perhaps she dropped her recorder and someone found it."

"What if Diego thought he could use the recording to bargain with the bastards to get Pilar back?" Luz mused.

"If so, he was not that frank with me."

Quin asked, "Who else is part of *La Liberación Humana?*"

"Th-that is not for me to say. If the wrong people found out—"

"We're not going to advertise," Quin said. "If you really want to help save Diego and Pilar, you'll tell us everything you know."

In the end, Jacinta's resolve weakened. She gave them the name and address of the vigilante group's leader, who had lost a younger brother the year before, plus the address of Pilar's mother in case they needed to speak with her.

Luz would gladly face the vigilante leader. It was the thought of facing the mother who'd lost her child that threatened to bring her to her knees.

QUIN WONDERED what angle he had to play to get Cesar Galindo to give him the time of day. He didn't believe that he could just introduce himself as an ICE agent and the man would talk. He decided to tell the truth.

Not wanting Luz to react in a way that would put off the vigilante leader, he told her, "Don't look surprised when I tell Galindo I was human trafficked into Mexico to work at hard labor."

She didn't get it. Didn't hear the truth of his words. But then why should she? In her eyes, he was a Special Agent for the federal government, a man in control, not a victim. He didn't want to think of himself as being powerless either, but the truth was the truth. He wasn't infallible. He didn't have superpowers—his most effective weapon was his brain.

They arrived at the address Jacinta had given them—a small house with a big yard at the edge of town. The yard was surrounded by a chicken-wire fence and a rooster strutted before a many-times-repaired hen house. The flat-roofed cement residence appeared to be in marginally better shape.

Quin parked the truck and went around to help Luz out but she was already out and closing the passenger door. He headed for the wonky porch, Luz following close behind, when the front door opened and a man with thick salt-and-pepper hair and mustache exited. Although he was wearing a loose gauze shirt, baggy cotton pants and huaraches on his feet, he stood tall and exuded a sense of power.

"If you're selling something, I don't need it," the man said in Spanish.

Quin asked, "Are you Cesar Galindo?"

"Who wants to know?"

"My name is Quin Farrell and this is Luz Delgado, the sister of Diego Ortiz."

The man pulled his face into a puzzled expression. "Hmm, Ortiz? Don't think I know him."

"You don't know he's one of the missing?" Luz asked. "Or that his girlfriend, Pilar Morales, is also?"

"Why would I know this?"

Ignoring his ploy to put them off, Luz continued. "We have missing loved ones in common. I know your brother was taken. I was taken myself when I was looking for Diego. I was placed in a brothel, threatened with my life if I tried to leave. I wouldn't be here if not for Quin."

"We were both victims," Quin said. "I was brought to a labor camp here in Mexico to work in the drug fields. I was lucky enough to escape, lucky enough to help Luz also. We fear Diego and Pilar may not be so lucky if we don't find them soon. We need information."

The man was silent for a moment, as if he were trying to determine whether Quin was telling the truth. Sensing his disquiet, his innate suspicion, Quin met his gaze fully, without looking away.

Finally, Galindo said, "What kind of information do you seek?"

"We know that Pilar spoke to Juan de los Reyes the day before he was murdered," Quin said. "Do you have any idea of what he told her?"

The man shook his head.

"She recorded the conversation," Luz said. "We think that's why Diego was taken—because they thought he knew where to find the recording."

"They who?"

"*El Jefe…,*" Quin said, "or his people."

"*El Jefe* is nothing more than a *rumor*, a ghost. No one has ever admitted to seeing him."

"That doesn't mean he doesn't exist," Quin insisted. "*El Jefe* has a cover that seems impenetrable. So what? Covers are meant to be broken."

Luz spoke up. "Plus, I may have seen him in the brothel where I was taken. His hair is unusual—glossy black with a thick streak of silver."

Galindo's expression shifted and he swore under his breath. "How do I know you aren't his agents?"

Quin asked, "Are you a man of faith?"

"I am a good Catholic."

"As am I. Faith got me out of that labor camp. Sometimes faith is all you can count on."

The man thought about it a moment, then nodded. In a low, threatening tone, he said, "But if you are not who you say you are, then know your life is worthless." His seething emotions receded a bit. "If Pilar confided in anyone, it would be Alma Marquez. You might find her at *Cantina Vida Loca*. Just tell her Cesar sent you."

CANTINA VIDA LOCA lived up to its name. Luz had expected busy and noisy and that's exactly what they walked into. The bar was low and dark—the single window having enough neon beer signs and a big "Girls" sign in red to keep out any sun. The male patrons seemed undeterred by the lack of light. They drank, they played pool or poker, they picked up the advertised girls showing off their wares in short shorts or microminis and halter tops at the long, hand-carved bar.

Luz saw an exchange of money—the guy put a wad of bills in a girl's top and got a feel out of it as well. Laughing, the girl curled her arm through his and led him off toward the blaring jukebox where she rocked her hips against his in an imitation of a dance. Luz suspected that wasn't the only rocking the woman was going to be doing to him tonight.

Suddenly, she felt an arm snake around her waist and pull her possessively against a rock-hard body. Wondering what in the world Quin thought he was doing, she gave him her best indignant wide-eyed stare.

"Just trying to keep you safe," he assured her in a low tone.

"From what?" In leaning closer to whisper, she brushed her breast against his chest. Trying to ignore the immediate discomfort, she asked, "You think someone's going to traffic me out of here?"

"In a manner of speaking." He nodded toward the gaming tables.

Luz followed his gaze to find more than one man eyeing her with interest even though she was conservatively dressed and made-up in comparison to the other women. Her stomach did a somersault. She leaned into Quin farther, splayed a hand across his chest as if he were her lover.

Well, in a way he was...

Ignoring her speeding pulse and the way her breath caught in her throat when she was this close to Quin, she asked, "So which one is Alma?" unable to keep her tone light as she switched her gaze to the half-dozen women left at the bar.

"One way to find out."

Quin lowered his head to speak directly into her ear, his breath making her skin pebble and her knees go weak. Despite the talk she'd had with herself about not getting any ideas about Quin—the last man she wanted to involve herself with was one who lived with violence—there were moments like these when she simply couldn't help herself.

"What's wrong?" he asked. "Are you having a change of heart?"

Realizing the girls at the bar were all working girls—and that she was the only female present who wasn't—Luz felt more than a little out of place. The reminder of what had almost happened to her trumped any attraction to Quin. She went cold and still inside. As if realizing it, Quin loosened his grip on her and gave her some breathing room.

In a low voice, she said, "I don't understand why Alma would choose this kind of life considering she's part of the vigilante group."

"Cesar didn't say that exactly. He said that if Pilar talked to anyone it would be to Alma. Undoubtedly she's doing what she's doing to keep a roof over her head and food on the table. There aren't as many options for poor women in Mexico to make a living as there are for us."

With that, Quin approached the bar. Luz followed, feeling eyes on her follow, too. Unable to breathe normally, Luz scanned the room to see who exactly was watching. The men for the most part had returned to their own amusements, although one swarthy guy with a scarred face aimed air-kisses at her.

Flushing, Luz flipped around away from him in time to hear Quin say, "I'm looking for someone."

The bartender was a young-looking kid with short dark hair and big dark eyes. It looked as if he'd borrowed his clothes from an older brother—both his shirt and vest were baggy.

Setting up shots, he said, "We have plenty of women. Take your pick."

"I'm looking for someone specific. Her name is Alma Marquez."

The kid immediately dropped the bottle he was pouring and bolted out from behind the bar to the front door.

"What's going on?" Luz asked as Quin started to move after him.

"Hell if I know, but I'm about to find out."

With that, he pushed through the crowd and out the front door.

Before Luz could follow, a man came up behind her and grabbed her by the wrist, making her heart jump and her mouth go dry as she turned to face him. It was the swarthy guy with the scarred face. He reeked of tequila and one of the scars pulled his mouth slightly to one side.

"Ain't you a classy-looking one?"

"Sorry I'm not what you're looking for," she muttered, trying to twist her arm out of his grasp.

"Who says?" he asked with a leer.

"I do. I'm not for sale."

Panic gave her strength. This time when she jerked her arm to free herself, she succeeded and before he could grab her again, she raced out of the bar after Quin.

# Chapter Nine

Quin caught sight of the bartender racing down the block, thin arms and legs pumping as he approached the corner. Not in as great a shape as he should be after being held prisoner for a month, Quin was nevertheless still fast. Whether he was fast enough to catch the guy before he disappeared was another question altogether. Narrowing his focus, he put on as much speed as he could gather.

The run took him straight down the block, the distance between them tightening only marginally. The bartender threw a look back over his shoulder and, seeing Quin, stumbled. A few lost seconds meant the gap shortened a bit more.

The guy raced around a corner.

Quin followed.

He was too far away to get anything off the guy—Quin needed closer contact to tune into his emotions—and so had no idea of why the bartender was running from him. Had something happened to Alma? Had the bartender been witness and now thought he was fleeing for his own life?

The street narrowed and several vendors were selling tacos and churros and hand-squeezed lemonade. The bartender tried to cross to the other side, but a speeding car slowed him again. With a frantic look over his shoulder, he ran sideways and knocked straight into a pushcart.

Fruit exploded in every direction.

"Hey, idiot!" the vendor yelled. "You're going to pay for that or I'm going to have you arrested!"

The guy danced to avoid stepping on the fruit. The vendor pushed him hard so that he went down on top of a sea of oranges and grapefruits and couldn't seem to get back to his feet.

Finally catching up to him, Quin reached down and grabbed the guy's shirt front to pull him up. With his free hand, he threw the vendor a twenty-dollar bill.

"For your trouble."

He didn't need the police involved.

"Let go!" the bartender yelled, thrashing to be free.

Quin simply picked him up by the shirt front and carried him away. It was only when he was setting him down and his hand hit something soft and full that he realized the bartender wasn't a he but a she.

Either that or the guy had some breasts.

"Let go of me! What do you want with me? I didn't do anything!"

A transference of panic flooded Quin. Incredulously, he asked, "You're Alma Marquez?"

Just then, Luz caught up to them and gasped, "He's Alma Marquez?"

"Not he. *She*." He looked back to Alma. "Why are you dressed like this?"

"I have no man to protect me and I don't want to be a whore. Working where I do, it's safer to be a man. What do you w-want with me?"

Realizing the woman thought they meant her harm, Quin let go of her and said, "Cesar sent me."

The name was enough to stop Alma from running if not to slow her racing heart. Quin didn't have to touch her to sense the way it drummed against her ribs. The intensity of her emotions receded only slightly.

"We're not going to hurt you," he promised.

"How can I be sure of that?"

Luz said, "Diego Ortiz is my brother."

"Diego?" Alma looked from Luz to Quin and then back to Luz. "Have you spoken to him recently?"

"Not since he set out to find Pilar and disappeared himself."

"Oh, no." Alma closed her eyes for a moment, then taking a deep breath, opened them again. "Maybe we should go someplace more private to talk about this. Come with me."

She led them to a nearby church.

The narrow interior was rife with the smell of incense, but there was no service going on. They were alone but for a woman dressed in black kneeling in a pew up front. She was too busy lighting candles and praying to pay them any mind.

Luz slid into a rear pew seat, Alma following. Quin chose the row in front of theirs and turned to face them.

"What is it you want from me?" Alma asked, her tone hushed.

Likewise, Quin said, "We know that Pilar was working with others to find the people who'd gone missing—"

"*La Liberación Humana.*"

Quin noted Alma didn't confirm or deny that she was part of the vigilante organization. He felt her continuing caution like a thick, impenetrable skin. He realized that while she might be talking to them, she wasn't altogether certain she could fully trust them.

"We know that Pilar got a lead on a witness she hoped would give her information about the human trafficking," Luz said. "We can't follow up on that because the man had an unfortunate accident."

Alma visibly shuddered. Inside she was roiling again. Quin could feel her distress.

He said, "Cesar thought Pilar might have told you what she learned."

Alma shook her head. "I don't know anything. I didn't want to know."

"There goes our only lead," Luz said. "Now what? If only we could figure out where she stashed that audio recorder. Or the tape."

Alma echoed, "Tape?"

"If it wasn't digital," Quin explained.

Alma shook her head. "There was no tape."

"So it *was* digital," Luz said. "Do you know the brand or what it looked like?"

"It looked like a cell phone."

"What?" Luz said.

"She recorded the interview using her cell."

"You're sure?"

"Of course I'm sure. That's what Pilar did. Does."

"So we're looking for a cell phone—"

"No! Pilar was always misplacing stuff or getting stuff stolen. She didn't want to lose the interview, so she recorded it and sent it to her own voice mail."

Quin exchanged looks with Luz. Perhaps they'd gotten a new lead after all.

"I need to get back to work before I lose my job," she said. "I want to stay on the safe side of the bar."

Quin swore under his breath. "I'm sorry. If you do get fired, I want you to call me." He handed Alma his card. "I'll make good on your loss until you can get a new job."

"Thank you."

"No," Luz said, "thank *you*."

They rose to leave the church.

"You'll find Pilar?" Alma asked. "And Diego?"

"We will," Luz said, and even though he had his own doubts, Quin didn't contradict her.

"If you think of anything else that might help, Alma, call me."

They walked out of the church together. Alma chose to run back to the cantina, while they took their time getting back to his truck.

"Is there some way we can get to Pilar's voice mail?" Luz asked.

"You mean legally?"

"I mean any way we can."

Luz's excitement was catching. If they could somehow break into Pilar's voice mail, they at least had a chance, however slim, at finding Luz's brother and his woman. Helping them might not make up for the tragedy he had caused, but at least it would be a start.

LUZ TRIED TO KEEP HERSELF centered as they made their way back to Quin's truck.

"So you can't get help from your office?" she asked.

"I could, but we'd need a subpoena to get at the phone records. That all takes too much time."

"What's the alternative?"

"Do you have Pilar's number?"

"Afraid not."

"Then I'm hoping her mother will give us her daughter's cell number, and I *really* hope she knows Pilar's password."

Luz wondered how likely that would be as Quin drove them across town to the address Jacinta had given them for Pilar's mother.

Situated in one of the better areas of the city, the large two-story cement house was painted blue with lime green trim. Luz forced herself to the front door only to find Señora Morales wasn't home. The woman who answered the door was elderly and wore an apron over her dress as though she'd been cleaning.

"Señora Morales went to the shrine to make an offering for her daughter's safety," the woman said, indicating the direction to take. "Two blocks this way, next to the flower shop."

Luz's stomach whirled at the small respite.

But when they arrived at the shrine, she felt even worse at seeing a woman who looked to be an older version of Pilar lay a bouquet of red roses at the feet of a skeletal statue draped in black. The woman wore black, too, including a shawl over her head. Even so, fine strands of gray were visible against her black hair, and her round face was unbearably sad.

The roses joined other offerings—flowers, tobacco, tequila—in front of what some people considered to be a saint despite the Catholic Church's denial. *Santa Muerte* or Saint Death was petitioned by many Mexicans who looked to recover health, stolen items or kidnapped family members. Photos of lost loved ones—mostly young women, some men, more children—lined the crown someone had set atop the grinning skull.

*Santa Muerte* was a figure that was revered both by ordinary people looking for solace and protection from the very criminals who also came to this supposed saint to pray for the death of their enemies.

The woman was praying in a low voice.

Nevertheless, Luz caught the reference to someone saving Pilar, and when the woman looked up, Luz could see her dark eyes, so like Pilar's, were wet with tears. A lump caught at the back of her throat. Quin gave her arm an encouraging squeeze so that she found her voice.

"Señora Morales?"

Wiping away her tears, the woman looked from Luz to Quin. "Do I know you?"

"I'm Luz Delgado and this is Quin Farrell. Diego Ortiz is my brother."

"Oh-h-h." Pilar's mother stumbled to her feet. "Has Diego found my baby?"

"I'm afraid not. My brother…Diego…disappeared while searching for her. Now we're trying to find what happened to them both."

As she'd feared might happen, Pilar's mother swayed, a muffled sound of horror escaping her. Quin caught and steadied the poor woman and kept her upright.

"I'm sorry…I'm sorry…"

"No need to apologize," Luz said. "I can only imagine how upsetting this is for you."

"But your brother, too…"

Luz fought the lump that suddenly seemed to fill her throat.

"Let us take you home," Quin said, and Luz was relieved when Pilar's mother nodded in agreement.

Even though Señora Morales was fairly young—probably not yet fifty—Luz noticed an underlying fragility about her, and she shuffled her feet like an old woman. Undoubtedly both were due to the strain of worry over her daughter. If they didn't find Pilar, Señora Morales would truly be old before her time.

During the quick drive back to her home, Quin explained that he was a Special Agent for ICE and that he'd been investigating the human trafficking in the area. He even showed her his identification to back up his story. Thankfully, Señora Morales didn't ask any further questions about Luz's involvement. Luz didn't want to have to recount the brothel situation.

When they walked into the Morales house, Luz noted the traditional hand-carved wooden furnishings, the woven carpets on the floor and the colorful artwork on the walls. All indicated the family had a good deal of money, not a surprise because Luz knew Pilar had gone to the university and that her father was a successful businessman.

The housekeeper was waiting for them. "I made tea," she announced, indicating the steaming pot and three cups on a low table before the living room couch and chairs.

Quin helped Pilar's mother to one chair, then waited until Luz took the other before he sat on the couch. The housekeeper poured their tea, then left the room.

Señora Morales picked up her cup but didn't drink. Instead, she cradled it between her hands as if she got comfort from the warmth of the contents. "How will you find my Pilar?"

Luz looked to Quin. He nodded, indicating she should take over. Not knowing whether the woman knew her daughter was part of *La Liberación Humana*, Luz said, "Her friend Alma thinks there's a message on her cell phone voice mail that might give us a lead. We don't have her phone number or her service or her password. We were hoping you could help us."

"I have her number and the service, yes, of course. But the password…" Frowning, Señora Morales shook her head.

"Maybe she wrote it down somewhere," Quin said. "If you don't mind our looking through her things."

"Anything to find her."

A single sip of tea and the woman insisted on showing them to her daughter's room herself. The room was large— a combination bedroom, sitting area and work area with a wall of shelves filled with books surrounding a desk and computer. Needing to see to her husband's dinner, Señora Morales gave them Pilar's cell number and told them to use the house phone.

Then she stood in the doorway for a moment, her emotions

transparent in her expression—hope warring with fear. Her whole body seemed to tremble.

"We're going to find them both." Luz connected gazes with Señora Morales, tried to feed her certainty to the poor woman. "My brother and your daughter. We're going to find them."

Pilar's mother nodded—hope winning for the moment—then left them alone.

Realizing she'd done all the reassuring, that Quin had remained silent as usual, she knew he wasn't as positive as she was. So then why was he there with her? Why did he agree to work with her to find them?

Not wanting to get into it, she merely asked, "So where do we start?"

"If you don't mind searching through her things, I'll take the computer files."

Luz didn't mind. She started with the dresser on top of which was a photograph of Pilar and Diego. Her brother's arms were wrapped around his woman and they wore smiles of utter contentment. Wondering if she would ever feel that with a man, Luz glanced back at Quin and caught him watching her while the computer booted up.

Warmth flooding her, she quickly turned away and opened the top drawer to find it filled with frilly, sexy lingerie that reminded her of the outfit she'd been forced into at the brothel. The outfit she'd been wearing when Quin…

Growing warmer, she quickly slammed the drawer and opened the next. It and every other drawer in the chest stored nothing but clothing.

No papers, no diaries, no secret passwords.

"Nothing there," she said, turning to see Quin tapping at the keyboard. "How about you?"

"I'm searching through Pilar's documents now for any file

names that jump out at me. Not that she'd have a file called *passwords*—but I was hoping something would stand out."

"What about her Internet passwords?" Luz asked. "A lot of people use the same passwords over and over."

"If I could get to them."

"Maybe you can…if you can get into her e-mail. Lots of people keep their registrations as reminders when they sign up for Web sites."

Luz crossed to the night stand. Inside the single drawer, she found a small book. Sitting on the edge of the bed, she paged through Pilar's diary, filled with observations about life, many about love—about Diego. No secret codes.

"Hey, I got into her Web mail," Quin said. "And there's a folder called My Stuff…" He paused for a moment, then said, "And here are registrations for various sites."

Luz replaced the diary and moved to the desk, where she stood behind Quin and watched as he searched file after file.

"Most are encoded, but apparently not all," he said, writing down the password.

Within minutes, he had three choices. All were similar combinations of letters and numbers.

"Why don't we try using these. We need the number she would call to pick up her voice mail from a land phone, though."

"I can get that."

Quin quickly found the number on the company's Web site and gave it to her.

"Okay." Luz picked up the phone. "I'll call the company's voice mail number and enter her cell number, then you read off a password and I'll enter that, too."

Which would have been a great idea if Pilar had used one of those Internet passwords. But one at a time, she was forced to eliminate them.

"Now what?" Quin mused. "Where do we go from here?"

Still staring at the keypad on the phone in her hand, Luz was focused and thinking about the number she'd used to call up Diego's voice mail.

"Hey, is something wrong?"

"Diego's password for his voice mail…7-4-5-2-7…"

"You think they might have used the same password?"

She shook her head. "Not exactly. 7-4-5-2-7—the corresponding letters are P-I-L-A-R."

"He used his woman's name as his password? Then what if—"

"—she used his?" A thrill shot through Luz. Her hand shook slightly as she dialed again, entered the cell number, and when the recording asked for the pass code, she punched in the number equivalent of D-I-E-G-O: 3-4-3-4-6.

She held her breath and hoped hard…

*"You have eighteen messages,"* the recorded voice said. *"To hear your first message, press one."*

"It went through!"

She pressed one as instructed, then quickly put the recording on speaker phone so Quin could hear as well.

The first three messages were simply friends trying to get through to Pilar. But the fourth message was from Pilar herself. They both listened to her drawing out Juan de los Reyes, encouraging him to talk.

*"Those men working for El Jefe will burn in hell for what they're doing to our people,"* he said.

*"You mean selling the services of women and forcing men into hard labor?"*

*"I mean killing them."*

*"How do you know this?"* Pilar asked.

*"I went across the border to get work. Someone told me that Hunt Ranch outside of Crystal Springs was hiring, so I went to see if they would hire me."* The man's voice was bitter.

*"Instead, I saw what they were about for myself—that the ranch was one of* El Jefe's *operations—and high-tailed it back here. I didn't want any part of that."*

*"What exactly was that?"*

*"Hunt Ranch wasn't named after a person. It's what they do. It's one of those expensive resorts where hunters can go after exotic game."*

*"There are a bunch of those in Texas…"*

The message suddenly ended and Luz pressed one to get to the next message. Diego calling Pilar. As were most of the remaining messages. Luz could hear her brother's calm peel away to be replaced by pure panic as he realized something had happened to the woman he loved.

Frustrated, Luz said, "I can't believe Pilar stopped recording when she did!"

"She probably ran out of recording time on her cell and didn't even realize it."

"Now we'll never know the rest."

"Unless we check it out for ourselves."

"You mean Hunt Ranch?" Luz asked. "I told you how I felt about killing animals. I am not even going to pretend to be a hunter."

"Neither am I. I'm going to pretend to need work."

Luz thought about it for a moment. "So you are going undercover?"

"That *is* my job."

"Then I'm going with you."

Quin shook his head. "It's too dangerous."

Not bothering to hide her annoyance, she said, "I thought we were partners."

"Aaron is my partner," he informed her coolly. "I let you tag along with me because I was afraid you'd get yourself into trouble if I didn't."

Luz gaped at him. Why this sudden turnaround in Quin's attitude? Or had he really felt this way the whole time? Had he been using her to get enough information to give him a lead to *El Jefe*?

"If you won't take me," she warned him, the words sticking in her throat, "I'll go on my own."

"Like hell you will."

His cold, stiff tone made her words flow out at him in a rush.

"You can count on my showing up in Crystal Springs, Quin Farrell! After everything we've gone through, you can't really believe I'll just go back to my old life and wait for someone else to find my brother!"

He took a step closer and gave her a tight smile. "Is that the real reason you want to go undercover with me?"

Suddenly having trouble breathing, Luz glared up at him. "What else?"

"You're attracted to me. You want to be with me, so you can try again."

"Attracted to you?" What an ego! And then his intimation hit her. "Try *what* again?"

Grinning, he ran a hand up her arm, sending a shiver through her. He couldn't really mean he thought she wanted to…good Lord, he did!

Luz pulled her arm free of his touch and smacked her hand into his chest. "Don't flatter yourself! Why in the world would I want a repeat of something so…so…"

"Scary?" He moved even closer.

Heat flushed through her and she was having trouble thinking straight. "Try *boring*!" Even though she knew her failure hadn't been his fault, she was desperate to get him to back off. "You wouldn't know how to please a woman if—"

She never got to finish. His mouth covered hers.

Even though she told herself to pull her head away, to stop

him before he sucked her in, she was powerless to fight him. He did unspeakable things to her mouth and she simply wanted more. Her pulse sped up and her heart hammered her ribs. When her knees went weak, she clung to him, every inch of her where they touched suddenly on fire.

He kissed her breathless.

And then he let go and stepped back.

She swayed and blinked in confusion. He was smirking at her!

"Boring?" he asked, raising an eyebrow.

Luz suddenly got what he was trying to do. He thought by scaring her with a show of virility, she would run in the other direction. His kissing her had the exact opposite effect—not that she was going to tell him.

Smiling as if she'd been the one controlling the situation, she said, "If you think that excuse for a kiss was supposed to deter me from going to Hunt Ranch with or without you, you have another think coming."

Flushing, he glowered at her.

"Keep in mind," he said, "we're going to do this on my terms or not at all."

"I can take whatever you throw at me."

Her words were more confident than what she was feeling. What if he actually did try to have sex with her again?

And considering how the last try had turned out, why wasn't that thought distasteful?

## Chapter Ten

They'd passed through customs and immigration and were on their way back to San Antonio, when Luz cried, "You want me to what?"

If he wasn't so serious, he would have smiled at Luz's outrage.

"Switching genders has been working for Alma." The very reason he'd gotten the idea of how best to protect Luz. If he hadn't been able to tell the bartender was really a woman, it would be possible to fool others. "If you do a good enough job at changing your looks, passing yourself off as a guy will work for you, too. And your pretending to be my little brother is the only way I'm going to let you come with me."

He thought she might threaten to go alone and so was surprised when she asked, "What about you? Aren't you going to change your looks so no one recognizes you?"

"Of course," he said. "It's all part of the plan."

Anyone could show up at the ranch—one of the men responsible for dragging him off to Mexico...one of the guards...Maribel the madam...*El Jefe* himself...

"So if I disguise myself as a man," Luz went on, "you'll disguise yourself as a woman?"

Ever since he'd kissed Luz, her tone had held an edge to

it no matter what he said to her, so he just backed off and took refuge in silence.

She'd been right—that kiss had been meant to scare her off. He figured after their disastrous night together, the last thing she'd want would be more of the same. So he'd tried to put that fear in her mind, hoping she would realize she was in over her head.

Instead, she'd responded to him with abandon and he'd been tempted to take her right there in Pilar's bedroom. Thankfully, he'd come to his senses. He didn't need to get any more involved with her than he already was.

Now what?

He was stuck with Luz Delgado—a brave albeit annoying albatross around his neck. He could bluff all he wanted, but in the end, he was responsible for her safety. An amateur could be trouble for him, could get him killed. Even if he backed out of his private mission, took Aaron's advice and just let it alone, Luz would no doubt plunge ahead without him. He would like to think he could set her up in Crystal Springs and go out to the ranch for work himself, but he didn't believe she would cooperate.

So he was stuck with her and with an uncomfortable situation of his own making. Just because he was beyond the McKenna legacy—beyond thinking he was going to find a soul mate like his siblings and cousins had—didn't mean he didn't have needs. That was all it was—physical attraction. No matter how bad an idea it would be, he couldn't help but wonder what it would be like to make love to Luz under different circumstances.

So she wasn't the only one on edge.

Quin could only hope that making her look like a boy would get his mind off what he fantasized doing to her.

Luz suddenly broke through his thoughts. "How long have

you been working at this—trying to bring down *El Jefe* and his operation?"

"Three years. Too long."

"Then why do you do it?"

"Because I'm good at it. Really good. Being able to sense things—whether or not someone is lying, for example—is a plus." The dreams sometimes gave him an edge, too, but they were never clear. And no one in the department knew about any of his psychic enhancements. Negativity whispered through him as he thought about the lack of progress in the case, but he had to keep focused or he would want to pack up and go back to South Dakota. "Someone has to take responsibility for helping people who can't help themselves. And if not me, then who?" The burden of responsibility never grew lighter. Or the guilt over not breaking the case sooner—the longer it took, the more people affected. He glanced her way. "Vigilantes?"

She flushed. "Obviously I can understand someone having personal reasons." Quiet for a moment, she suddenly asked, "Cesar Galindo's brother—would he have been abducted to be sent to a brothel?"

"Could be. But it's more likely he was coerced into some kind of bondage. Threats, violence and economic leverage such as debt often make a victim consent to his or her own exploitation. Worldwide, the revenue for human trafficking is estimated somewhere between five and nine billion dollars a year."

"My God…where have I been?"

"Living your life like most people do. It's not that people don't care. More like they hear these things on the news and either think it's all exaggerated, that it doesn't apply to them, or that there's just nothing they can do."

"I understand feeling helpless as well," Luz said, but she didn't sound helpless at all. She sounded determined. "So what will we call ourselves?"

Apparently she'd accepted his plan.

"How about Quique and Luc Chavez?" he said. "At least the first names are close enough to our real ones so we shouldn't forget them."

"Will we have papers?"

"Would someone who came across Rio Bravo to get work have papers?" he asked in Spanish.

She laughed. "Your accent isn't good enough to pass."

"Maybe not to a Mexican—"

"Not to me. If *I* can hear the difference, *they* certainly will."

Whoever *they* were. Would he at last come face-to-face with *El Jefe* himself?

"And should we speak in English," she went on, "it'll be even more obvious."

"You have a point," he agreed. "Claiming to be Mexican American would probably be safer anyway." She was already half there. "Which means I need to get that paperwork."

Using his cell, he gave Aaron a rundown of the plan.

"You're crazy, Quin, and I'd be crazy if I helped you. Come in and talk to Maria about this. You know she's not going to go for a citizen sticking her nose into our business."

The response not surprising him—Aaron always was more cautious than he—Quin asked, "How soon can you get the paperwork done for us?"

Aaron groaned but capitulated as Quin knew he would. "I'll need photos."

Quin agreed that once they'd under gone the transformation, he and Luz could take and transmit photos via his cell.

"If you can get them to me tonight," Aaron said, "I'll have a set of IDs for you by mid-morning."

"Will do." Quin closed the cell and set it on the console.

"What did Aaron say?"

"That we have some shopping to do tonight."

Once in San Antonio, they bought new clothes for Luz—running shoes and jeans and a couple of T-shirts, boxers and cotton shirts a couple of sizes too big. Even so, Quin wasn't sure the tops were big enough to hide her breasts.

"We need something to tie you down." He indicated where by waving a hand in front of her chest.

She flushed in return. "The right sports bra should do it—the cheap ones give you a real uni-breast look."

It was Quin's turn to be uncomfortable when she dragged him into another store and tried on several bras which she insisted he check out to find the one that worked the best.

To tell the truth, in his mind, nothing worked perfectly. Or maybe it was just the fact that he had a personal interest in her breasts.

They made a last stop at a drugstore to get hair coloring, scissors and a tanning lotion that didn't need sun to darken his skin. Although her mother was Anglo, her skin wasn't as pale as his, so she wouldn't need to alter it.

"Let's just pray this stuff doesn't make you look more orange than copper," Luz said. "That happened to one of my girlfriends in high school. I'm sure tanning products have improved, though."

They made their purchases and headed back for his truck.

"We'll go to my place," Quin said. "It'll be safer than yours. Whoever has your brother must know about you. And they got hold of your identification, remember, so they have your address."

"If they put two and two together."

"Do you want to chance that they won't?"

"No. Your place it is, then," she said. "No way they could know about you, right?"

"No way."

They couldn't, he was certain. When he'd been taken, he'd

been using fake IDs, so they didn't even know his real name—not even Bianca. No way would they be able to find him.

Once at his place, Luz took tags off all the men's clothing they'd bought for her while he shaved his face except for the stubble over his lip and on his chin. His facial hair grew fast enough that it would be filling in by morning. The only thing that worried him was the scar that cut through his right cheek. No way could he make that disappear without going through some elaborate ruse with makeup, which would be likely to come off at the wrong time. He would just have to hope he didn't run into anyone who recognized it—unlikely because it had been a guard who'd cut him when he'd been a prisoner in Mexico.

"Time for a haircut," he said.

"You want *me* to cut your hair?"

"I'm going to cut *yours*."

"What?" She gaped at him. "No way!"

"My way," he reminded her. "You agreed. Don't worry, it'll grow back."

He had to steel himself to the job. The feel of Luz's hair falling over his fingertips reminded him of the night in the wilderness, when he'd tried finding a way to make her relax and give over to the pleasure of a man's hands. He loved her hair. He hated cutting it all off. Then again, he would hate anyone figuring out she was a woman even more.

Afterward, when she looked in the mirror at hair that was shorn short on the sides and in the back and barely long enough to spike on top, her eyes filled with tears. He could see the effort she made to stop herself from crying.

"My own mother wouldn't recognize me." She met his gaze. "Your turn."

"My hair doesn't need to be cut." He'd had short hair when he'd been taken, so he had to look different both from then and from the night when he'd rescued Luz. "I'm going to tie it back from my face."

"Great," she muttered. "I get to look like a freak for months and you get to tie back your hair for a few days."

"You don't look like a freak. Just different." Truth be told, she still looked beautiful to Quin. "A few weeks and you won't remember why you were even upset."

"I shouldn't be upset over my hair. It's for my brother, so big deal, right?"

"Right. I'm going to need some help with that tanning lotion. My back."

"You want me to do your back?"

"What if I need to take off my shirt?"

She nodded. "All right. Give it to me."

He handed her the bottle.

The moment she touched him, he knew it was a mistake. Blood rushed to his extremities…all of them.

"These bruises," she said, lightly running her hand over his lower back. "Did you get them helping me escape?"

"Could be," he hedged.

He'd undoubtedly gotten the majority and more that didn't show being beaten at the forced labor camp. Not something he wanted to discuss.

She gently stroked his back. He took a big breath and steeled himself against the images she instigated. It didn't help. Every touch got to him, seared him until he was on fire. No matter how he tried to distract himself, nothing worked.

Thinking of his family reminded him of the legacy he hadn't yet fulfilled and wondering if there was some kind of catch, some way he could still end up with the kind of life Kate and Neil and Skelly and Donovan and Aileen and Keelin and Curran and Flanna had all found.

Why would he be the only one left out?

Thinking about past undercover operations brought him back to Bianca Ramos—the reason the legacy hadn't worked for him.

Thinking about the plan made him realize he and Luz would have to stay close—maybe too close for his comfort.

A hell of a situation he'd gotten himself into.

"What about your arm?" she asked, her hand stopping short of the bandage still covering the flesh wound.

He ripped it off. "Almost healed."

She carefully worked around the still-battered flesh. "What if someone sees it?"

"Either they'll think I'm someone to stay away from...or they'll think I'm one klutzy idiot. This scrape could have been from anything."

"Does it still hurt?"

"Just an occasional twinge. No biggie."

"Your getting yourself shot for me is a real biggie in my book," she told him. "If I can return the favor—"

"Don't. I'd hate to see you get shot. Don't try to prove you're as tough as I know you are. It's okay to let someone take care of you."

"I can take care of myself."

For the most part, that was probably true. "That's one of the things I admire about you. And one of the things that scares me."

"*You* scared?"

"You're an amateur, Luz. Gutsy and brave, but an amateur." He didn't want to consider what could happen to her if the wrong person saw through her disguise. What the hell was he thinking, leading her straight into danger? "You weren't trained to do what I do. You need to be more careful. You need to listen to me when I say back off."

"All right. I get it."

Remembering her threat to follow him, he thought maybe he should just tie her up and leave her somewhere safe. Not that he really would.

A moment later, she said, "There. Done. Unless of course you want me to—"

"What?"

"Go lower. Your, um, butt."

She said it with a straight face as if she didn't know how much she'd already affected him. The gleam in her eyes told him she wasn't that clueless.

"I can take care of my own butt, but thanks for the offer."

"Just trying to be helpful."

"I'll bet you are," he muttered, taking himself to the bathroom to finish the job.

"What about your eyes?" she asked, raising her voice so he could hear her through the closed door. "Blue eyes would be a dead giveaway."

"Not if they're brown."

"Contacts? You can get them by tomorrow?"

"I already have them. This isn't my first undercover operation."

After finishing with the tanning lotion, he cleaned up and popped the contact lenses in. Then he slicked back his hair and caught it with a leather tie at the base of his neck.

When he opened the bathroom door, Luz was dressed in the new clothing. She stood at a window and stared out into the dark. Her mind must have traveled someplace far away, because she didn't hear him enter the room or cross to her until he was at her side.

When she looked up, her eyes widened and her mouth dropped open. "Your own mother wouldn't recognize you, either."

He nodded. "Time for those photos."

After turning on all the lights in the room, he posed Luz against a blank wall.

"Try to look like a tough kid from the streets."

The expression she gave him made him want to smile. "Never mind. Change that to vacuous."

He didn't know what she was thinking about—maybe Diego and Pilar—but her silly expression turned sad, making him want to put his arms around her and tell her everything would be all right.

Instead, he took a picture.

"Your turn." He handed her the cell and traded places with her.

"Try to look macho," she directed.

Quin remained deadpan and she snapped the photo. After checking to make sure both would do, he sent them on to Aaron.

A moment later, he received a text message: *Got it. You could be on a WANTED poster.*

Good, then his work was done.

He flipped the phone closed. "We need to get a good night's sleep. Who knows when we'll have another chance? You can have the bedroom. I'll bunk out here on the couch."

"It looks way too small for you."

"I've slept on worse," he said, thinking of the cell floor in the labor camp. "Go to bed."

Luz nodded but didn't make a move.

"Something wrong?"

"You keep giving me warnings." She paused a second, then asked, "This is going to work, right?"

"Keep your head down, don't look anyone in the eyes and you'll be fine."

"Not me. I mean Diego. What we're doing…we're going to find and rescue him? And Pilar?"

Hoping that it was true for her sake, he said, "We'll do our best."

His goal was to shut down *El Jefe's* operation and make sure he got the justice he deserved. And if they could rescue Diego and Pilar, he was all for it.

*If* they could.

Surely Luz knew it could already be too late.

*"You think changing the color of your eyes and skin was enough to fool me?" Bianca asked, walking around him, touching him as if trying to brand him as her slave.*

*If he wasn't chained to the floor again, he might have gotten up and strangled her. "What gave me away?"*

*She shook her head. "I knew you the moment I saw you."*

*"I don't believe you."*

*Bianca laughed. "Good for you. You believed me last time."*

*"My mistake."*

*"You thought I was something I never was."*

*"Desperate and in need of rescuing?"*

*She laughed again. "I let you have me so I could learn the truth about you. And I liked the things you did to me." She trailed her fingers along his neck. "One last time?"*

*"No!" he said, but she was already on him, trying to arouse him. He fought her, threw her off him. "Get it through your head—I don't want you, so stay the hell away from me!"*

"All right!" Luz gasped, getting herself up from the floor where he must have pushed her. "I get it! It's just…you were making noises like you were in pain. Sorry I bothered you."

Before she could scurry back to the bedroom, Quin caught her wrist. "Luz, wait." His head was clearing and he realized he'd mistook her for a dream. "It wasn't you…I had a nightmare… sorry…didn't mean to push you away."

"Yeah, okay."

"Did I wake you?"

"I couldn't sleep. Strange place, strange bed."

"I'd warm up some milk—that's what my mom used to do for me when I couldn't sleep—but the fridge is empty."

"No problem."

But Quin could see there was in the wetness of her eyes. Could hear it in the stillness of her voice. Could feel it in the emotional vibrations she gave off. Guilt…fear…uncertainty. He read them all in her.

He told her, "It's not too late to change your mind."

"Is that what you want?" Luz asked. "Me to back off? That would be easier for you, wouldn't it? Then you wouldn't have to consult anyone else. You could just do what you want and hell with the consequences."

"Are you willing to back off?"

"I'm willing to do whatever I need to on my own, if necessary."

He shook his head. "You'd just get in the way."

"How do I know I can trust you, Quin? You want *El Jefe*, but without me to be your conscience, how concerned would you be with finding my brother? Diego's my priority. I've gone through the last several years of my life without any real purpose. I've hidden from the tough stuff." She shook her head. "Not this time. I have to do this. Maybe if I'd been paying better attention, this never would have happened."

"You're giving yourself too much credit." Wondering what she'd been hiding from, he added, "Too much to feel guilty about."

"Don't you ever feel that way?" she asked, as if she could read him.

The image of that poor guy being riddled with bullets when

trying to escape with him suddenly came to mind. "Yeah," he said tersely. "It's what drives me."

"Then we're on the same page."

Except of course that, despite being held captive for a couple of days, she was still pretty much a virgin when it came to the kind of experience he'd had.

"Go to bed. Try to sleep."

She stared at him a minute before saying, "Come with me. I'll feel safer with you close."

"You want me to come to bed with you."

"Just to sleep," she clarified. "It'll be better for you, too. Trying to sleep on a couch that's too small would give anyone nightmares."

Despite the fact that he knew this was a very bad idea, Quin got up and followed her into the bedroom. Luz crawled onto the bed and when he followed, she set a pillow lengthwise between them.

Grunting, he settled down, and despite Luz's closeness, his body relaxed the moment it hit the mattress.

He shouldn't be so comfortable with Luz. He hardly knew her. How did he know she wouldn't turn on him to get what she wanted? She wasn't Bianca, he told himself, wondering what the hell tonight's dream had been trying to tell him.

That for some reason Bianca wanted him?

It couldn't be that. Too direct. He knew very well that the dreams weren't just dreams. They were warnings. He should be used to their hidden messages by now…

So why couldn't he read beneath the surface this time?

He lay there in the dark, listening to Luz's breathing grow deeper until she was asleep.

How far could he trust her? he wondered, his cynical side suddenly engaged.

The dreams altered his perceptions and would continue to

confound him until he figured out what they meant. What was the message the universe was trying to get through to him? He was done with Bianca, but she kept making guest appearances. Could she simply stand for something?

A woman's betrayal?

Would Luz betray him if it was the only way to rescue her brother?

Once the thought occurred to him, he couldn't shake it.

# Chapter Eleven

Her own mother wouldn't recognize her. That certainly was the truth, Luz thought, taking a last-minute look at herself in the truck's sunshade mirror.

"Stop worrying. And stop checking yourself out. Guys don't do that."

"Thanks for the tip," Luz said drily. As if she would advertise her nerves with other people around.

"You look fine. Keep the hat on and slouch a lot and no one will pay you any mind."

Is this what women had to do to be safe from being trafficked into a brothel? she wondered, thinking about Alma, certain the possibility had factored into her decision to dress like a man.

Until meeting Alma, her sole concern had been the safe return of Diego and Pilar. But Alma's dressing like a man to be able to work safely had made her stop and think about the plight of the poor. Especially about the women who were working in brothels against their will, like the ones she and Quin had left behind while escaping. When the feds had gotten there to shut down the place, they'd been gone.

But to where?

Pilar had gotten Juan de los Reyes to admit that trafficked

people were being killed. What if that had been the fate of the women at the brothel?

The potential for such violence frightened her…and made her angry.

She thought about all those people recruited into various forms of slavery by coercion, deception or fraud. Abduction wasn't the only means of taking advantage of the poor. Where would it all stop? And who could stop it, really? As Quin had said, it wasn't that people didn't care, but that they figured there was nothing they could do about it.

But not him.

Quin had to be the most heroic man she'd ever met. He lived his life fully. She didn't want to acknowledge the violence he encountered on a regular basis, but she admired the fact that he didn't hide from any situation, no matter how tough. To her shame, after Gus had been killed, she'd hidden from anything unpleasant.

It had taken a personal reason to break her out of hiding, and after they found Diego and Pilar and freed them, Luz didn't know what she would go back to. She wanted her own life to have purpose.

Like Quin's did.

And yet not.

The level of violence that he considered a part of his work scared her to death. At times *he* scared her to death. She couldn't be like him, not after this.

Couldn't be with him, she knew, a part of her saddened by the thought.

They passed the sign that announced they were entering the town of Crystal Springs, Texas, Population 1,832. Luz noted they were on Main Street, the buildings mostly of Spanish architecture, others of limestone without the orna-mentation. Side streets wheeled off the main drag, commercial buildings quickly giving way to homes, all old, many tired-looking.

Quin pulled the truck into a gas station and stopped the truck at the pump closest to the building. "I'm going to fill up, then go inside and ask if anyone in the area is looking for workers."

"Why not just get directions and go straight out to Hunt Ranch?"

"Might not be the best way in," Quin said. "Better to have a recommendation from someone here."

She watched him via the side-view mirror for a moment.

The Quin she'd come to know seemed to have disappeared in his guise of Quique Chavez—cowboy boots and jean jacket, brimmed straw hat and sunglasses. And somehow, he looked more fierce than usual.

Could he really put on a new persona as easily as he changed his clothes?

Or was something simply eating at him?

Remembering the nightmare he'd had, Luz wished she could just ask him what that had been about. She simply didn't feel comfortable enough doing so. Even though they'd slept in the same bed the night before, he'd been terse with her all morning.

With the heat pervasive through the windshield, she opened the window to let in some air. Leaning out the window, her stomach knotting, she looked around to see if they'd raised any interest, but no one paid them any mind.

Just as Quin replaced the nozzle at the pump, the station door opened and a middle-aged man wearing a Stetson over his shades and carrying what looked to be an expensive hand-tooled leather satchel exited the store.

"Sir, excuse me!" Quin called. "Do you have a minute?" He flipped his persona again, gave the man a cheese-eating grin that took Luz by surprise.

The stranger stopped in his tracks. "What's it you need, son?"

"We need work, my kid brother and me." He indicated Luz in the truck. "Know of anything to be had around here?"

"Mmm, not in town, but the big ranches always need hired hands. Can you cowboy?"

"Yeah, sure, some."

Luz watched Quin act like he was half-exaggerating, when she knew very well he could probably outride anyone of her acquaintance.

"What about the kid? Is he legal?"

"We're both born and bred Americans, sir!" Luz shouted in the throaty voice as close to male as she could get.

"I mean age. You look young."

"I'm seventeen."

When Maribel had suggested she say she was twenty, she'd thought *that* was a stretch. But Quin had insisted.

"He's a good worker," Quin said anxiously.

The man studied Luz for a moment. Feeling as if she had worms crawling in her stomach, she studied him back.

He finally turned to Quin. "There's the Blackwell Ranch, about twenty miles east."

"That the only one?"

"Well, no. There is another ranch..."

It was obvious to Luz that the man was reluctant to recommend it, but Quin didn't give up so easily.

"We really need to make some money, sir, no matter where we have to go. My brother and me, we gotta eat, you know?"

"Not a matter of distance, son. Hunt Ranch hasn't been the same since it was bought up a couple years ago."

"What makes it different?" Luz asked, and for her trouble, got a warning glance from Quin.

"Used to be one of the finest cattle ranches around." The man shook his head. "Now they're more interested in taking people on hunts. Exotic game."

Though her chest tightened at the thought, she said, "We need work real bad, mister. We don't got anyplace to go."

The man sighed and shook his head. "Okay, I get it. At the far end of town," he said, indicating the direction, "take the road west about ten miles. You'll see a Hunt Ranch sign. Then you take the gravel road all the way in, maybe another seven or eight miles."

"Thank you, sir." Quin jumped to shake his hand. "Mr...?"

"Cooper. Dan Cooper. People call me Coop."

"I'm Quique and this is Luc."

"Good luck to you both."

Luz waited until the man had walked away to his vehicle—a luxury SUV—before saying, "Not exactly a recommendation."

"But at least we have a name that should get us in the back door."

With that, he went inside to pay. When he came out it was with a couple of cans of soda. He handed her one, popped the top on the other and took a long drag before starting the engine again. The cold soda was more than welcome. Even though it was spring, it was almost scorching. Mid-afternoon, it was probably in the high-eighties.

"So Mr. Cooper doesn't approve of Hunt Ranch. Do you think he knows people are dying out there?"

Quin shook his head. "He's a decent sort. If he knew, he wouldn't have mentioned it unless it was to say stay away at all costs."

"How do you know he's decent? You can't tell what he's thinking."

"More like what he's feeling."

Luz stared at him, expected him to snicker or something, but when he remained serious, she said, "You're not kidding, are you?"

"Nope. Part of the legacy from my grandmother."

"Legacy—that sounds romantic."

"Trust me, it's an inheritance that's far from romantic. More like a curse at times."

"So you can tell what anyone is feeling?"

"Some people are less open than others, but yeah, pretty much."

"Me?"

"You're easy. You wear your heart on your sleeve."

Not wanting the details—had he sensed her growing attraction to him?—she dropped the subject. That didn't keep her from thinking about it, though, wondering what he might have surmised about her.

"There's the sign," Quin suddenly said, slowing the truck and turning onto the gravel road.

The words *Hunt Ranch* were in big, blood-red letters, and below it, *Home of Exotic Hunts*. Between the lettering were the heads of animals—puma and javelina and nilgai.

Luz shuddered and only hoped she wouldn't be witness to death of any kind. Hard for her to believe that seeding an enclosed area with game that people could come in and shoot was considered a sport by anyone.

They arrived at the ranch proper soon enough. The house was stone, two stories with a balcony above the covered porch. Nearby were several other buildings—barns with corrals, storage buildings, living quarters for the workers, plus what looked like fancied-up quarters for paying guests over to the east side of the property.

Also extending beyond the barns and corrals to the west were several pastures, each holding a few grazing horses.

Quin pulled the truck under a live oak away from the house. A few vehicles—an SUV, a truck and a convertible—were scattered under another pecan tree, and a couple of pines.

"Let's head over there," he said, pointing to an occupied corral, "find out who's in charge."

The hair on the back of her neck raised slightly and she furtively scanned the grounds as she followed Quin. Was someone watching them, maybe from the house? Not wanting to appear suspicious, she didn't dare turn around to find out. Instead, she hunched her shoulders and caught up with Quin.

A Pinto, obviously unbroken, wouldn't keep a hand who was trying to ride him on his back. The man hit the dirt hard enough to unseat his hat and send up a cloud of dust to cover him all the way up to his balding head.

Another guy sitting on the top rail of the fence, blond hair poking out from beneath his billed cap, laughed. "Hey, Carl, that's showin' him."

"I'd like to see you get your fancy butt up on this one, Bobby Ray."

Quin zeroed in on him. "Hey, excuse me, Bobby Ray. We're looking for work. Who do we see?"

His expression hostile, the man eyed them both up and down. He spat out a wad of tobacco on the ground next to Quin's boot and said, "We ain't got no work."

"Not what I heard. You the bossman?"

Luz noted Carl got off the ground, pulled his hat down hard on his head and approached the horse.

"Who you been talkin' to?" Bobby Ray asked.

"Coop. Dan Cooper."

The man grunted. "What can you do?"

As Carl was unseated as fast as he mounted, Quin said, "I can ride that horse, for one."

Bobby Ray's mouth stretched out and Luz thought that was one evil grin. She shivered inside.

"I wanna see this. Carl, we have ourselves a real cowboy here. He's gonna ride Old Jughead."

"Hah, let's see him try!"

"If I ride him, will you hire us?" Quin asked.

"You have to stay seated and ride him all the way around the corral."

"No problem."

"What about *him?* What can he do?"

Before Luz could answer, Quin said, "Anything I tell him to do. Kid's just learning, but he's game."

"Can you ride?" Bobby Ray asked Luz directly.

Pulse suddenly rushing as she thought he might insist she ride Old Jughead as well, Luz said, "Passable. Nothing fancy like him, though."

Quin was in the corral now, and Carl took a seat on the rail next to his buddy. "Go ahead, get on him!" he urged. "What're you waiting for?"

Focused on the horse, Quin didn't answer. Instead, he whistled as he'd done with the horses at the brothel. Difference was, those horses had been broken, Luz thought. The Pinto rolled his eyes and backed up and the two hands on the rail laughed some more.

Luz glared at them, then focused back on Quin who was whistling softly now, getting the attention of the horse whose ears twitched and eyes rolled and nostrils flared. Quin kept going for him, the whistle shifting into low words she couldn't hear.

The Pinto quieted some and Quin put out a hand. At first Luz thought the horse might bite it, but in the end, it looked more like a nuzzle. The eyes stopped rolling, seemed to focus on Quin and whatever it was he was murmuring. The ears were pricked as if the horse was listening hard.

Luz's mouth dropped open as it hit her—he really had a gift of being able to communicate with animals.

Another part of his grandmother's legacy?

It made sense. If he could really tell what people were feeling, surely he could do the same with anything that had a heartbeat. But in this case, he seemed to be able to make the horse understand him without speaking.

Could he do that to another human being?

Quin ran his hand up the Pinto's nose, straight between the eyes. The horse lowered his head until Quin was whispering in his ear. Then he rounded the horse's head and mounted without any fuss.

"What the hell!" Carl grunted.

At first the horse appeared startled and confused as if trying to decide how best to unseat Quin, but Quin kept talking in that low voice, running his hand over the Pinto's neck until he settled.

After which, he rode the horse all the way around the corral. *Three times.*

Dismounting, he offered the reins to Carl. "By the way, his name isn't Old Jughead. He prefers Skywalker." When Carl didn't immediately jump down, he said, "You can ride him, now. Just go easy on his mouth. So who do we see about a job?"

"You're lookin' at him. Bobby Ray Martin, foreman of Hunt Ranch."

"Enrique Chavez. Call me Quique. And this is my kid brother, Luc."

When the foreman turned his attention to her, Luz looked down at the guy's boots, nodded and grunted.

"He legal to work?"

"I'm seventeen!" Luz said, trying to sound indignant.

"Yeah, but you're a small one."

The next thing she knew, Bobby Ray's hands were all over her, feeling for nonexistent muscles in her arms.

"Hey!"

"Not hey…hay," Bobby Ray corrected her. "The kind you're gonna deal with in bales. You'll work in the barn, muckin' the stalls, feedin' the horses." He shook his head and spat out another wad of tobacco. "Mmm, I don't know."

"I'm tougher than you think," Luz said. "I'll surprise you in the end."

She wasn't talking about how strong she was. If Bobby Ray Martin had anything to do with her brother's disappearance, she would certainly make sure he paid.

Not that he got her drift.

Quin got it, though. Probably he was reading her again. All those times he stared at her like he was looking inside her— now she knew why.

"Yeah, all right, I just lost a man and I was already short-handed, so I'll give you two a week to prove yourselves."

Luz dearly hoped they wouldn't need a week to either find Diego or learn where to find him. The longer it took, the less likely they were to have a positive outcome.

"All right. I'll show you where you can bunk," Bobby Ray said, moving away from the corral. "You'll have some time to settle in before supper."

"Is that when we get the paperwork?" Luz asked as he walked right on by the bunkhouse, making her wonder where he was taking them. "You know, tax forms and such."

"No paperwork. You're off the books until you prove yourselves. We keep you, then we'll go through all that government rigmarole. You don't got any objections, do you?"

"No," Quin said. "None."

Luz wondered if it was really a way to save some work if things didn't go well, or if the paperwork was never done. That way there wouldn't be proof of who exactly worked on the ranch. Then if someone who'd never filled out the government forms should disappear…

"Where do we start and when?" Quin asked.

"Daybreak. Coffee's on at four, setup on the porch outside the bunkhouse kitchen. Breakfast is at six or whenever you finish cleanin' out the stalls and giving the horses their feed."

"All sounds doable," Quin said.

"There's a lot more to do—like mendin' pasture fences—the horses are just for starters." Bobby Ray stopped outside a cabin at the edge of a wooded area. "I suggest you fill your bellies tonight. You'll need the fuel in the morning."

Luz was taking a good look around at the isolated area. She could see a couple more cabins in the distance and wondered who was staying in those.

Quin said, "Pretty nice. Here I'd thought we'd get nothing more'n a couple bunks with the other boys."

"Hunt Ranch doesn't have as many hands as it did when it was strictly runnin' cattle," the foreman said. "The herd is tiny compared to what it used to be less than a year ago— mostly for local consumption—so we need a lot less men. Less men, more room, so the boss figures it makes happier workers if they can spread out some, have a little privacy."

"The boss…who would that be?" Luz asked.

"Why, Mr. Hunt, of course."

But Coop had told them there was no Mr. Hunt, that the name of the ranch was significant of the ranch's purpose rather than a family name. Even through the dark lenses of his sunglasses, Quin's gaze burned her. She connected with him, then looked back at Bobby Ray.

"You can bring your truck back here," the foreman said. "Might as well stop and get linens while you're at it. Go to the back door, and see Betty—she's the cook and house-keeper—and tell her I said to set you up."

"Anything else we should know?" Quin asked.

Bobby Ray shrugged. "Just keep to business. Keep your noses out of anythin' that doesn't concern you, and it'll be all good." He started back out the door.

"We'll be along in a minute," Luz said. "I gotta use the facilities."

Bobby Ray didn't so much as look back.

The moment he was out of earshot, she asked Quin, "What do you think?"

"Hard to tell. He's not the most likable sort, but that doesn't make him guilty of anything."

"What does your psychic whatever-you-call-it tell you?"

"That he plays close to the vest. I didn't get anything off him because there was nothing to read. He was operating in neutral, so to speak."

"Even if he isn't guilty, he probably knows something. I don't see him talking, though."

"Me, neither. We can't count on anyone talking."

"Then how are you going to run this investigation?"

"By exploring this place thoroughly tonight and seeing what I can find."

Luz quaked inside a little at the thought of getting caught where they weren't supposed to be.

*Keep your noses out of anythin' that doesn't concern you*, Bobby Ray had told them.

And if they didn't? What then?

But if they didn't, how would they ever find Diego? It was possible her brother was here somewhere on this very ranch. Pilar as well. Which meant they had to search the property without getting caught.

A rush of panic shot through Luz as the improbability of actually finding her brother and his woman here on ranch land occurred to her.

"Take it easy," Quin said, cupping her shoulder and rubbing it as if trying to soothe her nerves. "Don't go jumping to any conclusions."

"How did you…"

Luz didn't finish. No doubt he was *reading* her again. Despite the desperation of her thoughts, she felt warmth spread through her at Quin's touch. It lit all the dark places in her and made her wish they'd found each other at a different time, when there wasn't so much at stake.

Without Diego's life being at stake, they wouldn't be together now. Reminded of the violence she had so far survived, she pulled away.

And once free of Quin's intimate influence, she told herself they would never be together at all. Perhaps she didn't want to hide in her bookstore any longer, but that didn't mean she wanted to expose herself to constant danger, a given where Quin was concerned.

"I'll just be a minute."

She headed for the facilities, had to use cool water on her face to calm herself down. It was her concern for her brother that was making her so nervous, she told herself.

But when she came out and Quin took a turn, leaving her to stare at the bare bones setup—a small wood table and chairs, an upholstered chair and one bed, barely big enough for both of them—she knew that was a lie. No room to put a pillow between them tonight. No matter that she knew he wasn't for her, her insides did a dip and turn and she took a deep breath to steady her suddenly roiling stomach.

Would they have at it again despite her good sense? she wondered, pressing her thighs together. Just the thought of having a second sexual encounter with Quin made her warm all over. Surely she could put the violence he served out of mind for a short while…

The bathroom door opened and Quin's footsteps trod heavily across the plank flooring. "Something wrong?"

Flushing, Luz turned away from him and moved toward the door. "Just thinking," she said, hoping he couldn't read her right now.

They headed back for the truck, but as they approached the house, she said, "Why don't you bring the truck around to the back door and I'll find the housekeeper."

"Deal."

Luz cut through the rear door into a mud room. From there, she could either enter the kitchen or a hallway that led to a staircase. She took a good look from where she stood and memorized as much of the layout as she could see.

A woman with frizzy brown hair and soft curves worked in the kitchen, adding spices to a big pot. Her face was round and unlined, her expression naturally cheerful. She looked to be in her mid-forties. Suddenly she grew aware of another presence and looked up at Luz with a welcoming smile.

"Well, don't just stand there, boy, c'mon in. I'm Betty, the cook. And you certainly need some fattenin' up. Hungry?"

"Um, actually," Luz said in her best low guy-voice, "the foreman said you would get us the linens for our cabin."

"Us?"

"Me and my brother. I'm Luc Chavez. Quique's bringing the truck around."

Suddenly two scary-looking Dobermans rushed from the front of the house through the kitchen and straight at Luz, who froze, heart in mouth.

"Knock it off, Brandy and Tequila!" Betty said. She gave them a sharp whistle and hand gesture.

The dogs sat, but they didn't take their eyes off Luz. They stared at her like they were wondering if she would make a good meal between them.

"They're a little territorial," Betty said. "They'll be okay when they get to know you. Hang on a minute, honey, and I'll get you those linens."

Wanting to know how big the staff was, Luz reminded herself to keep her voice low and husky when she asked, "So you do all the cooking and the cleaning?"

"I do now. Not so many mouths to feed and the owner don't like too many people wandering around the house."

"Sounds like you've been here a long time…since the previous owner?"

Betty nodded. "And glad for the work," she said, sounding a little tense.

Did she know what had been going on here lately? Luz wondered. That people had died? Could a normal person really stay and work for someone who had people killed?

Hoping not, hoping Betty wasn't necessarily loyal to the new owner, Luz wondered what she could get out of the woman. "What's the new *patron* like?"

"Mr. Ward keeps to himself mostly." Although she sounded disapproving, Betty added, "That's all right. I know I'm too talkative for most people."

"Not for me," Luz said, thinking they'd hit paydirt with the cook. "I get lonely away from home. Nice to have someone to talk to other than my brother."

About to probe into what Betty knew of this Mr. Ward, Luz bit her lip when the woman said, "I'll get you boys those linens now."

She disappeared down the hall. Luz would have liked to follow, to get the lay of the land, but the dogs stood between her and the rest of the house. That they didn't take their eyes off her made her skin feel a little prickly.

Luz heard a deep voice coming from the front parlor. A man was speaking, his words too low to make out. Was he on the phone? She listened harder, but Betty returned, carrying an armload of bed linens and towels and Luz still heard the voices.

"Here you go, then."

Luz took the towels and sheets and scraped out a "Thanks" in a gruff voice.

"Consuela used to be the housekeeper, but Mr. Ward fired her for no reason and left running the house to me."

Luz figured she knew the reason—Consuela was probably Mexican and the owner didn't want divided loyalties considering what seemed to be going on here—and then hoped that Consuela really had lost her job rather than her life. She couldn't forget what Juan de los Reyes told Pilar.

The front door slamming made her realize she was just standing there, thinking.

"My brother's waiting for me," she said, "so I gotta get going."

"See you at supper, then, six sharp. The dining room for the hands is in the old bunkhouse."

Luz smiled through her disappointment. "See you there."

She'd been hoping to get back in the main house to get more of the layout. She supposed she ought to leave that to Quin.

That and the Dobermans.

# Chapter Twelve

Quin was pulling the truck around to the back of the house when he saw a man dressed in an expensive suit take the steps down to the walkway two at a time. He slowed the truck so he could get a better look—and noted the wide silver streak in the guy's hair before a Stetson covered it.

Hell, that had to be the guy Luz had seen in the brothel! The one she thought might be *El Jefe!*

Quin stopped short of the back door and craned around to get a better look as the man got into the convertible and started the engine. A woman was already ensconced in the passenger seat waiting for him—the man leaned over to kiss her. As the convertible swung around, Quin got a fast glimpse of braided dark hair and an exotic profile below big sunglasses before the car whipped down the gravel road.

Stunned, Quin sat there, unable to move, unable to think. Had he really seen her?

"Hey, the least you could do is open the door."

Realizing Luz was standing outside the truck, arms full as she waited for him to give her a hand, Quin leaned over and opened the passenger door.

"Can you take this stuff so I can get in?"

He took the pile of linens from her and pitched them to the backseat.

Luz climbed in and settled down. "What's up? You seem a little out of it."

His mind suddenly racing, Quin said, "I thought I saw someone I knew."

"Where? Who?"

"Front of the house. In the convertible. The driver was a man. He had dark hair with a thick silver streak."

"He must have been the one I saw in the brothel! The man I thought was *El Jefe!*"

"Exactly. When he drove off, I got just a glimpse of the woman…but she looked like Bianca Ramos."

The possibilities of why Bianca might be at Hunt Ranch with the man who could be *El Jefe* raced through his mind as he drove toward the cabin in silence. Halfway there, he realized Luz was staring at him.

"What?"

"You look like you've seen a ghost."

"No ghost. A real, live woman who was trafficked up from Mexico. One I tried to help."

If only it was that simple. His gut was knotted and his throat felt tight. And he wasn't even certain it was Bianca he had seen. What if his mind was playing tricks on him?

"So what happened? The woman, I mean."

"She betrayed me. I guess this—living here in a decent place—was her reward."

"I'm missing something."

Quin stopped the truck in front of the cabin. Rather than going inside, which at the moment would feel like another jail cell, he headed for a fallen log under some nearby pine trees. At least out here he could breathe.

Luz followed. "Quin, how did this Bianca betray you?"

Quin never thought to tell her about it, but as he dumped

himself onto the log, the words tumbled from his lips as if he had no control over them.

"Bianca was human-trafficked into a brothel like you were. I, um, was using her to make my case, but I got a little too personally involved and told her why I was there and that I could get her out. I was about to break her out when the guards overpowered and drugged me. Before I passed out, I heard enough to know she had turned on me. It was obvious that she was trying to protect herself by telling them I was an ICE agent."

"How horrible," Luz said, sitting next to him and touching his arm as if trying to console him.

He concentrated on that one spot of warmth, because he suddenly felt very cold inside. If that had been Bianca in that convertible...

Luz broke into his thoughts. "I'm so sorry. What happened then? Did they try to kill you?"

Her outrage wrapped around him and when he looked at Luz, her eyes were blazing. "They dumped me in Mexico," he told her, "on a drug production farm. They kept me drugged and chained...and beat me if I wouldn't work..."

Luz sucked in her breath. "So the story you told Cesar Galindo was true."

He nodded. True as far as he'd told it. He didn't know that he could ever share with anyone the truth about his escape.

"This Bianca...how personally involved were you? Did you..." She hesitated a few seconds before finishing. "...fall in love with her?"

He heard an off-note in her voice, sensed the tension stiffening her shoulders. She cared, Quin realized. For some reason she cared how he'd felt.

He said, "I thought she was *the one*."

"Oh."

"You don't understand." Quin pulled a hand over his face. He'd never talked about this with anyone, not outside the family, but for some reason, he wanted Luz to know. "Part of my grandmother's legacy—*act selflessly in another's behalf and my legacy will be yours*—had to do with love, with finding a life-partner. And it was the right time—I was the right age. All part of the legacy, if you believe in that sort of thing."

"Obviously you do."

He couldn't tell if Luz did as well, but at least she was listening openly. "I'm the last of nine cousins," he said. "The holdout. The only one of us who hasn't found a soul mate and started a family." And despite an occupation to the contrary, a family was something he'd always wanted. "Obviously I'm the exception to the rule."

"You really believed it was going to happen, then."

"Considering the stuff I've been dealing with since I was a kid—my connection to animals, being an empath, the dreams—"

"Whoa. Precognitive dreams?"

He realized he hadn't explained that part, even though Luz had been witness to one of them. "Right. Unfortunately, they never make sense. They're like puzzles and there's always a piece missing. If only I could figure out why I'm dreaming about Bianca…"

Luz's confused emotions blanketed him for a moment, but she drew them back and hid them before he could read her.

Not knowing why he felt the need to explain his own feelings, he said, "Bianca is an untrustworthy woman, Luz, I know that now. Now I feel nothing for her other than hatred for the way she turned on someone who was only trying to help her."

"What if you *did* love her?" Luz said, her tone flippant.

"None of my concern."

But he thought she was concerned.

Part of him didn't want her to think he was hung up on another woman…while the other part thought it was for the best. He'd only known Luz Delgado for a few days. They were connected by the human trafficking situation. Nothing more.

Why should he care what she felt?

For some damn reason he did.

"Listen, I have no soft feelings left for Bianca Ramos. It was just seeing that woman took me back to the worst month of my life. Come to think of it, she probably wasn't Bianca, just another woman with similar looks, and I jumped to the wrong conclusion."

"If you say so."

Luz didn't sound convinced.

Quin couldn't convince himself either. He had to find out for certain, but that would have to wait until later.

He rose and said, "Let's get those linens and our bags and set up the cabin before dinner."

Meanwhile he would have to figure out a way to get into the house so that he could discern if the woman *was* Bianca. His only uncertainty being what he would do to her if the woman who had sent him to a living hell really was living here at Hunt Ranch.

SUPPER IN THE BUNKHOUSE was done. They'd all eaten together at a single long plank table. In addition to her and Quin and Bobby Ray and Carl, there were only three other hands. Curiously enough, after having heard Pilar's interview with Juan, the workers turned out to be all Anglos.

So where were these Mexican workers who were being killed? Luz wondered. Had the word gone out so that no one who was Mexican would look for work here? She only hoped that was true. She also thought they needed to get a better look at the entire property and wondered if they could accomplish that in one night.

"Let me help you get some of this stuff back over to the house," she told Betty, knowing they were going to start at the house later, after everyone was asleep.

"Thanks. I appreciate it." The cook finished loading the dishwasher. "Even though we have a small kitchen set up here, I can't be in two places at once. Just easier to do the actual cooking for everyone in one place."

"Does Mr. Ward have a big family?"

"None at all. At least not immediate. Well, not that I know of." Betty added detergent, then closed the dishwasher door. "If he does, they're not here. No, there's just him and his guest to feed at the main house. And tonight neither of them ate here."

So the house was empty, Luz thought, wondering how long that would last. And how to get the information she wanted from the woman who'd been here before the current owner. Again she wondered how much loyalty Betty had for this Mr. Ward.

Pretending she didn't know different, Luz asked, "Would his guest by any chance have dark hair with a silver streak?"

Laughing, Betty started the dishwasher. "Stars, no. You must have gotten a look at Mr. Ward himself. The guest is his lady friend."

Luz wanted to ask the lady friend's name, but she figured that might be pushing it a tad. Maybe a more natural way to find out the woman's identity would come up.

"You haul the stew pot and I'll get the rest," Betty said. Indicating the pot on the stove, she rounded up the big salad bowl and the basket which had held a couple dozen biscuits, all of which had been consumed.

"Sure, no problem." Still half-full, however, the pot was heavier than Luz had guessed.

As she followed Betty out the door, Luz glanced back to see Quin talking with one of the hands they'd met at supper.

Even so, his eyes followed her every move. He had no clue as to her plan—to get back into the house and make as much of a mental map as she could to make things easier for them later. Quin had some surveillance electronics he planned on installing in the dead of night.

An activity that would preclude any intimacies between them, Luz thought, telling herself that was as it should be. They were here on a serious mission, not to have fun. Assuming she could find fun in bed. That was still up for debate.

As if Betty was clairvoyant, she said, "You ought to get yourself to bed early tonight." Then added, "Work around here starts at the crack of dawn."

Although Luz feared they might not get any sleep at all, she said, "So I've been warned."

"Where did you work before here?" Betty asked as they crossed to the main house.

"Just on the family spread."

"Well, whatever are you doing here, then?"

"Let's just say that I, um, had no choice."

Which was true, Luz thought, grateful that Betty didn't pursue it.

They entered the house and Betty set the salad bowl and bread basket on the counter. "Just leave the pot right there." She pulled a plastic lidded container from a cabinet and a large spoon from a hook. "Dang. Where is my head? I put my car keys down somewhere in the bunkhouse and then forgot about them. I'm going to have to go back or I won't get home tonight."

"I can unload that pot for you," Luz offered, taking the spoon from the cook. "No big deal. Go find your car keys."

"Thanks, Luc, you're a good kid." Betty opened the mud room door. "If anyone gets home, I'll be right back."

Still enough time for her to take a quick look around, Luz thought. Feeling only a little guilty that she'd fooled the woman, she quickly scooped the stew from the pot into the container and place it in the refrigerator.

But as she started down the hall for the front parlor, paws slapping on the staircase stopped her.

The Dobermans!

How had she forgotten them?

Even as they hit the floor and rounded the stairs, her pulse sped up and her chest went tight. Cursing under her breath, Luz backed up and wondered if she could bribe the dogs with some stew.

Deep growls warned her not to try it.

"Sit," she said, gesturing the way she'd seen Betty do. "Brandy and Tequila, sit!"

The Dobermans kept coming. And growling.

Wanting in the worst way to run out of the house, Luz didn't dare turn her back on the dogs. As she passed back from the hallway into the kitchen, she looked around wildly for a likely weapon she could use to stave them off.

"Hey, Luc, what's taking you so long?"

Hearing Quin's deep voice suddenly come from the mud room made her heart skip a beat and her knees go weak.

"Um, it's the Dobermans," she choked out. "They don't want me to leave. Heh."

The dogs' gazes suddenly shifted to a spot over her right shoulder and she knew that Quin was there behind her. He didn't say a word, didn't even whistle like he had with the horses, and the next thing she knew the dogs were whining through their noses.

And sitting.

"Handy trick," she choked out, her pulse slowing.

With a light touch on her arm, he urged her backward. "Go on, get out of here."

She did, looking back only once to see Quin stooping and

the dogs sliding forward, their heads low, as if they were sub-servient to him.

Then she was outside and breathing normally again and the next thing she knew, Quin was beside her. "What the hell were you thinking?"

She took a quick look around to make sure no one was in hearing distance. "That I could get a better look at the layout while the lights were still on and everyone was out of the house. I forgot about the dogs."

"They're all right." He took her arm and moved off in the direction of their cabin. "They won't bother you again."

"What? You gave them instructions?"

"Something like that."

"What's it like, being leader of the pack?" she asked.

"Normal. For me. It's not that I'm their leader—I just have a way of connecting to them. It's always been this way ever since I was a kid."

"With every dog you meet?"

"Not all dogs...but in general, most animals."

"Good, especially if we're going to take a look in the woods, see what surprises might be hidden there."

He nodded. "Maybe later. Now there might be interested eyes watching us."

"What are we going to do until we can get back in the house?"

"A couple hours of sleep might not be a bad idea. I can set my cell phone to wake us." He nudged her. "There's your cook."

Indeed Betty was coming their way if on the opposite side of the bunkhouse. The cook held up her car keys and Luz gave her a thumb's up as they passed each other.

Quin had a way of connecting with people, too, at least with her. Every moment they spent together—whether fighting or plotting—Luz felt more and more drawn to him. The attraction went beyond personal magnetism.

No matter how the job ripped him apart—no matter how much violence was involved—Quin was completely dedicated to his mission.

A reason to admire him.

And to stay as far away from him as she could.

"You're acting as look out, that's it," Quin said, when they set out shortly after midnight.

He'd slept for nearly three hours on the floor, giving Luz the bed to herself this time, although he wasn't sure how much rest she'd gotten. He didn't want to think about the ideas he'd had before falling asleep…

Quin removed the spy ware from a secret compartment under the backseat of his truck. He'd parked up in between the cabin and a stand of firs. The truck was three-quarters hidden from view. Only the nose stuck out of the natural shelter. He and Luz were completely hidden from anyone's view.

"You remain outside and keep watch," he went on. "And stay out of sight."

"What if I see someone coming?" She sounded a little on edge. "Do I whistle or what?"

"No, just tell me. Softly. You're going to wear this," he said, holding up a tiny, wireless mike. "Open your shirt."

A shaft of moonlight poked through the branches, just enough so that he could see her fingers shaking as she undid the buttons.

Even though she was wearing a sports bra under her T-shirt, Quin had a difficult time not reacting as he lifted it to hide the mike. The back of his hand brushed her warm stomach and he felt her flesh quiver.

"It's painless, I promise." He clipped the microphone in place. "There. Done." And quickly withdrew his hands.

Luz just as quickly pulled her T-shirt down and buttoned the cotton shirt.

When he secured another mike to himself, she said, "So I'll be able to hear you, too?"

"Absolutely. We can have a meaningful conversation while I wire the place."

He handed her a compact earpiece while he donned his own.

The rest of the equipment—more wireless mikes and a couple of wireless cameras—went in a ditty bag that he was able to carry under his jacket.

"Ready?"

"As I'll ever be."

He led the way along the tree line, wanting to stay out of sight for as long as possible. When they passed the bunkhouse, he was extra careful, just in case Bobby Ray was hanging around. Not that Quin thought he bunked down there. Undoubtedly he had another cabin, one farther into the woods. Something Quin would have to check out later.

When they drew even with the house, he whispered, "Stay there," and kept going until the front of the house was in view.

Only a single car was parked under a pecan tree. No sign of the convertible. He studied the house itself. Lights were on up front on the first floor. Probably the front parlor. What looked like a night-light shone from a single window above.

He moved back to Luz's side. "Stay here. I'll be as quick as I can. You see anyone, hear anyone, just whisper a warning."

"Got it." Quin took a thorough look around to make sure no one was in sight before taking off. He hesitated before crossing the open area next to the house, waited for a cloud to cover the moon. Then he made his move. If luck held, he'd be in and out of the house before the owner and his woman— whoever she was—returned from their night out.

## Chapter Thirteen

It wasn't long after Quin disappeared into the shadows that a sense of unease whispered through Luz.

She checked the road but saw no vehicle lights.

Still, she couldn't relax. With Quin so close and yet so far from her, she hadn't slept. Maybe her nerves were due to her growing exhaustion. She did a one-eighty, scanning every inch of the area slowly and thoroughly, yet saw no movement anywhere.

So why was her skin crawling?

A breeze whipped through the trees sheltering her and skittered down her spine. The sound was layered with something else.

Footsteps?

That was it! She'd been hearing stealthy footfalls against the soft earth and now they were coming closer.

Too close to warn Quin?

She heard a growl—a roar?—and the low cadence of a person's voice.

Definitely too close.

The path to the house was momentarily moonless. Her heart thundering, Luz threw a fast look over her shoulder to make certain the threat wasn't close enough to see. Then she edged toward the house and made a quick dash across the open space.

Only when she was in the shelter of the building did she dare take a full if shaky breath. She gave her nerves only a second to steady before softly gasping, "Quin, I'm outside the door. I'm coming in."

Even though this part of the house was dark, she knew the Dobermans were waiting for her. They growled and advanced on her, but a soft whistle made them trot back down the hallway.

She followed, whispering, "Quin, Quin, where are you?"

Quin intercepted her at the parlor entry. There was just enough light for her to see his angry expression as he asked, "What the hell are you doing here?"

"I heard someone—"

"I told you to stay put!"

Did he really think she was messing around? Fear escalating her temper, she returned, "I couldn't say anything to warn you because they were too close!"

"They? There were two of them?"

"I'm not sure how many men. I heard a man's voice and a growl."

"A dog?"

"A big cat."

Swearing under his breath, he swung through the parlor to the office beyond. "I'm not quite done. Get back into the kitchen and keep watch."

"All right!"

Luz turned on her heel, the Dobermans following, making it difficult for her to breathe again. Even though she'd never been afraid of dogs before, she was making an exception for these two. She swallowed hard and kept watch through the kitchen window as Quin had ordered.

At first it seemed as if the threat was over—as if whoever

was out there had kept going or had retreated. But then one of the dogs got to his feet, the other quickly doing the same. Both stared intently at the back door.

Then Luz caught movement outside—someone coming around the corner of the house.

"Quin, we have to get out now."

"Come this way. Hurry!"

She got down the hall just as the back door opened. The dogs were whining and a man was talking to them, but her heart was beating too loudly for her to make out what he was saying.

The next thing she knew, a hand covered her mouth and an arm wrapped across her chest and pulled her away from the front parlor. Knowing it was Quin, she relaxed and let him do what he wanted with her, then found herself pressed up against the wall on the other side of the staircase, his body sheltering her. She knew very well that if the person entering went up these stairs, he or she couldn't fail to see the two of them unless the light stayed off.

The dogs' nails clacked along the hallway in their direction and one of the Dobermans hesitated at the foot of the stairs. Her eyes having adjusted to the dark, Luz saw him poke his nose in their direction. Quin used a hand signal to make the dog move off and join whoever was in the parlor now.

Listening intently, Luz heard two sets of footsteps continue on, probably into the study.

Suddenly Luz realized she was drowning in Quin's heat, with his big body still pressing her to the wall. Getting her hands between them, she flattened them against his chest and pushed. It was like trying to push a wall. Frowning, she looked up and met his gaze, which prompted a tingly hot sensation from her center to her toes. She blinked and tried to shake away his influence, but being so close to the man left her feeling oddly helpless. Half-heartedly, she tried to push him again.

He gave his head a sharp shake and then redirected his attention to the other room. That he wasn't so intent on her let her breathe a little more easily. She could barely make out the deep voices coming from the study—so there were two men.

Could Quin hear more clearly than she? Was that one of his *gifts*?

Suddenly he pulled back, freeing her, and she nearly dropped from the wall, catching herself on him. Her breasts brushed his chest and the intense sensation popped her back against the wall. If he was affected, he didn't show as much. He raised an eyebrow and tapped his forefinger to his lips. She nodded and let him ease them from the tight space. They moved around the staircase. The light from the other room spilled into the hallway, so it was easier going.

The voices were louder now, but still not clear enough to catch the conversation between the men. Appearing mesmerized by whatever was going on in the other room, Quin indicated she should go before him. Was he able to make out what the men were saying? she wondered.

Luz slid silently down the hall, taut nerves making her misstep. Thankfully she caught herself before banging into the wall or landing on the floor.

And then Quin was right there, directly behind her, using an arm lightly across her back to guide her. The touch made her pulse race even faster.

What the heck was wrong with her? How could she be so unfocused, let her attraction to Quin distract her like this? Or maybe it was the danger that intensified how she felt when close to him.

*Danger and the threat of violence…*

The cool night air felt soothing against her heated skin. It also cleared her mind. She let Quin take the lead back toward the cabin, stuck to him like glue until they arrived there safely. And then she felt she could breathe easily again, at least for a while.

Quin went directly to the truck and his spy ware under the rear seat. "That conversation was recorded," he said softly, throwing some switches and pulling out a mini-LCD monitor.

The next thing she knew, she could see the men—the supposed Mr. Ward with Bobby Ray—and could hear them through the earpiece she was already wearing.

*"You still haven't gotten the bastard to talk?"* Ward asked.

*"Not for a lack of tryin'. Took him out yesterday, let him see what was what for himself. I told him he could be next."* Bobby Ray cursed. *"Nothin'!"*

*"He knows that's an empty threat. If we kill him, we'll never get the damn recording!"*

Realizing what that meant, Luz gasped, even as Ward continued.

*"Hmm, there's still the woman."*

*"If she didn't break yet,"* Bobby Ray said, *"what makes you think she will now?"*

*"I mean use her. If he thinks she's the one who's gonna die…"*

*"I'll get her and see what I can do tomorrow. I like the way you think, boss."*

And then they changed the subject.

Luz collapsed against the cabin, sank down and let tears roll down her cheeks. "He's alive. Diego's still alive. Pilar, too. Thank God we didn't get here too late." Although she'd refused to consider the possibility, it had been at the back of her mind throughout.

"We still have to find them." Quin was putting away the equipment. "But at least it sounds possible."

Which reinforced Luz's opinion that he hadn't really believed it before.

"At least Diego is here," she said. "It sounds as if Pilar is elsewhere…maybe one of the brothels."

Sadly for her and for her brother, Pilar might not be the

same woman she had been less than two weeks ago. Knowing Diego—how he'd never given up on Pappa—Luz was certain he wouldn't give up on Pilar either. No matter what happened to her, he would make sure she knew she was loved and could count on him.

If they both got out alive.

Tears of relief still filling her eyes, she got to her feet and found herself wrapped in Quin's comforting arms. For a moment she gave over to raw emotion and let herself rest against him. His hand traveled down her spine, as if he were stroking her like he would a cat. Closing her eyes, she fisted the front of his shirt.

But when she felt his lips brush the top of her head, she looked up at him questioningly.

Shards of moonlight cut through the trees and she could see his face clearly. His expression was intent, his gaze fixed on her. She could hardly breathe again, not from fright this time, but from something equally scary. He lowered his head—slowly enough to give her time to back off—but she waited, breath now bated to see what would happen.

This kiss was no challenge, no means of frightening her off as it had been the last time. This kiss was warm and comforting and filled with a need she shared.

For a moment, she forgot why she shouldn't be doing this with Quin.

For a moment, she forgot he was everything she feared in a man.

Standing on her toes and sliding her arms around his neck to better anchor herself to him, she kissed him back with fervor. He made a noise deep in his throat like the growl she'd heard earlier—wild and primitive—and pushed her back against the cabin wall. He cupped one of her breasts, thumbed the nipple through the layers of cloth. The sensitive flesh responded, sending a network of pleasure through her.

For a moment, she indulged herself.

For a moment, she forgot everything but her deepening connection to this man.

And then she came to her senses.

*Diego...*

Panting, Luz pushed Quin away. No matter how she felt, what she needed physically, she had to remember that Quin lived with the kind of violence that had made her go underground for nearly five years. She couldn't stand it. Plus, she needed to stay focused on finding her brother and his woman. Anything else and they could be too late and then she never would forgive herself.

"The other cabins," she gasped. "We can start with those."

Quin stood in her way and didn't move. Didn't say anything for a moment. Simply looked like a man coming out of a trance, awakening to the reality of their situation.

Finally, he said, "You need to get some rest."

"I need to find Diego."

He scowled at her. "I can move faster alone."

"Then we can go our separate ways."

"How much sleep did you get before?"

"None, but—"

"No buts. You need to sleep."

Even though she knew he was right, she argued, "I'll sleep for a week after we find Diego and get him out of this place."

"Have you always been this stubborn?"

"Have you always been so block-headed?"

Quin's scowl deepened at the escalating argument. "If you don't stop and breathe, you're going to break."

"What's it to you?"

He shrugged. "I would hate to see you crumble under the pressure."

"Who said I will?"

"It would be a miracle if you didn't."

A low roar cut through the night, making the hair on Luz's arms stand straight up. "That's the cat I heard before. I'm sure of it. I know this place takes hunters out for game…but why would a mountain lion come in this close?"

"I don't know, but it's another reason for you stay tight in the cabin. If there's a big cat roaming the property, I can deal with it." He cut off any further objection by saying, "Remember you agreed to let me be the boss of you if I let you come along. And I'm ordering you to stay here and try to sleep. I promise I will check out every building on the property before I come back."

The moment she said, "All right," exhaustion swept through her and she longed to close her eyes if just for a minute. "What if you find where Diego's being held?"

"It all depends. If I think I can take care of any guards and get him out, I will. Then we'll come get you and get the hell out of here."

The thought of Quin in another violent situation made Luz shudder. "You'll be armed, right?"

"I'm always armed."

The thing she needed to remember.

No matter how attracted she was to him, Quinlan McKenna Farrell wasn't for her.

He might live with violence.

She wouldn't.

WHAT THE HELL was he doing, messing with Luz Delgado? *Focus, man!* he ordered himself.

He checked the cabins, the quarters that must be intended for wealthy guests, the buildings that held farm supplies. He scoured the area, saw nothing out of place, saw no guards stationed anywhere that would trigger his suspicions. He caught a glimpse of Carl once, but it looked like the man was checking the perimeter. And then he disappeared.

So, defeated for the moment, Quin went back to the cabin to regroup and maybe get another hour or so of sleep before having to get up and play barn hand at dawn.

To his relief, Luz was fast asleep.

Quin couldn't bear Luz's disappointment when he told her he'd struck out. She'd been so hopeful. But there was still reason for hope. The ranch was huge and any illegal activities undoubtedly would be kept out of sight, away from workers who would talk and especially away from paying customers. He hadn't missed the Mercedes outside of the fancy guest quarters.

He would simply have to find a way to explore more ranch territory. He'd figure it out in the morning. But now he needed some shut-eye.

Still, he didn't immediately drop to his bedding on the floor. He couldn't help himself. He stood just staring at Luz for the longest time, feeling…what?

A connection.

A need so bad it hurt.

An indecision.

She looked young and innocent and beautiful beyond belief. He had no idea of how she fooled any man into believing she was his brother. Despite her hair being so short and her breasts being in bondage, she was every inch a woman to him.

One he was beginning to care about more than he wanted to admit.

He shouldn't have kissed her. That had been worse than making love to her that first night, because now he knew her. And he knew better than to use her badly. The McKenna legacy was out of his reach. He hadn't met her in time, so she couldn't be the one.

What did it matter that he wished differently?

Luz Delgado was the fiercest, bravest, most loyal of women—and would make any man proud to call her his own. He wanted to think she would make his grandmother Moira proud. If only it wasn't too late.

He threw himself down on his bedding, determined to get some sleep. But the legacy kept playing itself over and over in his mind.

*Act selflessly in another's behalf and my legacy will be yours...*

*"Your legacy will be the death of you."*

*A gun barrel circled his neck, making his skin crawl.*

*She was behind him, taunting him, trying to make him see the error of his ways.*

*"You're a fool. You have such hope. Despite everything, you think you can win."*

*"Why can't I?"*

*"Because you see what you want to see, not what's really there."*

*"What is there?" he demanded to know.*

*"You have to do more than open your eyes to see the surface," she taunted. "You have to open your mind to recognize what's underneath."*

*Laughing, Bianca walked away, his own confusion leaving him tied in knots and unable to go after her.*

# Chapter Fourteen

The bizarre dream must be responsible for Quin's thinking he saw Bianca first thing the next morning.

When Luz stepped in the bathroom to shower—trying to hide her disappointment that he'd seen neither hide nor hair of her brother—Quin stepped out of the cabin to fetch a couple mugs of coffee. That's when he spotted Bianca coming out of the guest quarters, wearing jeans and a white shirt, her black hair flowing down her back to her waist.

*He remembered that hair...*

Before he could see her face, she rounded a corner and disappeared from sight.

Quickly, he took off in that direction, seeing a blur of movement between buildings. He moved faster, rounded the corner and almost ran into a worker who was carrying a laundry basket filled with linens. She was young and pretty and had dark hair, but she wasn't Bianca Ramos.

"Can I help you?" she asked, sounding fearful.

"Sorry. I'm new." He held out his hands, palms facing her, in a gesture of peace and backed up. "Just looking for the morning coffee."

"Over there." She pointed the way.

Quin tipped his brimmed hat and moved off, all the while

turning in circles and searching the area for another woman. If Bianca was really there, though, he didn't catch sight of her.

The dream, he told himself. That dream had really messed up his mind.

"*Open your mind to see what's really underneath,*" she'd told him.

Did that mean she was hiding here under false pretenses? That Ward/*El Jefe* didn't know who she was or why she was there? For revenge?

Unfortunately, that didn't make any more sense than his thinking she might be *El Jefe's* woman.

Fetching the coffee, he brought it back to the cabin where Luz had just stepped out of the shower. She was fully dressed but had that glow about her that made Quin's gut tighten.

He held out a cup of coffee. "Here's some gas for the tank."

"Thanks. Now I can wake up." She took a gulp then glanced down at the floor. "Did you sleep at all?"

"Enough."

"We could have shared the bed."

Quin merely grunted, took a slug of coffee and kept his thoughts to himself. Share the bed? Without doing something about his bed partner? Not likely.

"So what now?" she asked.

"Now we get to work, earn our keep."

"I mean about Diego."

He told her what he had in mind.

They spent the next couple of hours mucking out the barn and hauling out the waste in wheelbarrows, swept the aisles and fed the horses.

Then they went to breakfast to feed themselves.

The breakfast was set out buffet-style, big pans over warmers. This morning the cook was nowhere in sight.

"I never thought I could be so hungry," Luz said in a low voice. "I could eat a snake."

He'd just bet she could—as long as she didn't have to see it killed. She had a tender heart for any living creature. Heaping his plate full of eggs and biscuits and sausage, Quin sat himself down at the plank table next to Carl.

"How did Skywalker do after our go-round yesterday?" Quin asked the man. "Is he performing for you?"

"He lets me mount 'im, but he's still a jughead, far as I can tell," Carl grumbled. "Don't want to go when I get 'im out of the corral."

"I can take him out and work him," Quin said, as if he didn't care one way or the other. "See if I can figure out what's holding him back."

Carl looked at the foreman for permission. "Bobby Ray?"

"Yeah, sure. Let's see how many miracles Quique here can pull out of his hat. If you manage it, I have a few other jugheads that need some training on a bit, too."

Quin shrugged. "No problem. I'll get started right after breakfast."

"I can go with," Luz said, "ride one of the other horses."

"Not you. I have a stall that needs disinfecting."

"I'll look forward to that."

Bobby Ray laughed. "I see your little brother has a sense of humor."

"It's how we get through the day."

Quin dug into his food and tried not to show his triumph at putting his plan into action. Luz kept a neutral face and didn't let her disappointment slip through.

She amazed him in so many ways.

Everyone ate fast. Quin ate faster, wanting to be saddling up Skywalker while the other hands were having their morning smokes. When he finished, Luz left her food half-eaten, and he knew it was because she wanted to talk.

"Can we wire up?" she asked softly when they were out of hearing distance.

"Not a good idea unless you want to take a chance on giving us up. Too many things can go wrong."

"I just wish we could stay connected."

"I promise I won't leave without you."

"That's not what I meant."

A soft note in her voice revealed worry for him. About to tell her that he could take care of himself, he bit his tongue rather than throw her worry back in her face.

That kiss had changed something between them...

Skywalker was pastured near the barn. Quin whistled and the horse came to the fence. Quin slid through the boards and mounted bareback. Giving the horse some leg, he looked to the gate. A moment later they were through it and in the corral outside the barn.

When he went to fetch the tack, Luz was already divesting the stall that needed sterilization of its old bedding. She worked like she'd been doing it all her life and he remembered her saying she'd grown up on a ranch.

She must have sensed him staring at her because she turned around. Even though she was wearing a brimmed hat, enough of her face was open to him that he could see the hope shining through her fear. He didn't make promises he couldn't keep, but he gave her a thumbs-up sign anyway. Quickly she ducked her head and even from this distance, he could feel her. She was sad and hopeful, scared and elated. And she was fighting tears.

Quin took his leave and tacked up Skywalker and rode him out as fast as he could. The sooner he found Diego, the sooner they could get out of here and the sooner he could think about whether or not they could be together when this mission was completed.

LUZ waited until everyone was hard at work before making for the cabin. She'd disinfected the stall and had laid out fresh straw, but she wasn't about to alert Bobby Ray to the fact. The less contact she had with the foreman the better.

Where was Quin now? Had he found the place where they were keeping Diego?

If only she could have gone out with him, surely they would have found her brother by now.

Once inside the cabin, she cleaned up fast, then went out to the truck. She didn't know how long she had before someone would come looking for her, but she was going to take advantage of every minute.

Thankfully the rear of the truck was hidden from prying eyes. She could briefly check the camera feed and any digital recordings and hope they got some evidence on what was really going on here.

She would continue to pray that Quin found Diego and was able to free him.

After making sure she was alone, she opened the compartment under the truck's back seat, pulled out the equipment and turned on the monitor. She flicked the scene from one camera to the other and stopped when she got to the one directly across from the desk in the study.

The woman sitting at the desk was concentrating on the computer to one side. She was barely in profile and her long, loose dark hair got in the way, so Luz couldn't get a good look at her face.

So, had Quin been correct? Was this really Bianca Ramos, the woman who had betrayed him?

Luz couldn't help her churning emotions—a combination of disdain for the woman and fear that Quin would still find her tempting despite his assurance to the contrary.

No matter that she switched to other cameras, Luz couldn't see what was on the screen. She wondered if Quin would be able to somehow enlarge it when he got the recording back to the office. She knew that the cameras had motion sensors and started a digital recording every time a camera turned on.

Wondering how long the woman had been in the office, Luz found the remote and took the recording back to the moment she'd stepped into the office.

Bianca hadn't been alone.

Bobby Ray accompanied her and seemed to be very deferential, as if taking orders.

Wanting to hear what they were saying and not having her earpiece handy, she took another quick look around to make sure no one was close by before she put the volume on low.

*"Listen, Bianca, I went to get her, but the woman was already gone,"* Bobby Ray was saying.

*"What? What are you talking about?"*

*"She escaped somehow. I don't know how we're going to get that recording."*

Good Lord, they were talking about Pilar!

A better look at Bianca direct on made her catch her breath. The woman's Aztec features were familiar. Luz was certain she'd seen them before. But where? Could Bianca have been a model for one of the ceramic faces of the missing women on display in Jacinta's shop?

*"I'll have to take care of it myself, then,"* Bianca was saying. *"Tonight."*

*"How?"* Bobby Ray sounded disbelieving.

*"Let's agree that I have a way with men. I can make him tell me what I want to know."*

There was no mistaking Bianca's meaning, Luz thought. She meant to try to seduce or trick Diego into talking. Is that what she had done with Quin? Luz wondered. Slept with him so that he would confess to being an ICE agent?

If true, that meant Bianca never had been in danger…that she had been part of the operation from the beginning…that she had purposely set up Quin.

*"The client coming in late tonight is very particular,"* Bianca said, *"but very wealthy. And bored as so many of them are. He wants one of our ultimate hunts."*

*"We don't have no stock on hand."*

*"Of course we do."*

*"But what if you don't get the location of the recording from him first."*

*"Don't worry, I will."*

*"But what if you don't?"* Bobby Ray insisted. *"With his woman gone, you have no leverage."*

Dear Lord, he meant Diego! Bianca had referred to her brother as stock!

The ultimate hunt…hunting prey with equal intelligence …another human being!

Is that what Juan de los Reyes had been telling Pilar when the recording had cut off? When he'd said people were being killed?

They were being *hunted* like wild animals?

*"I will get what we need from him."* Bianca lifted a hand to brush back her hair from her face.

Luz glued her gaze to the bracelet on Bianca's wrist—a gem-studded, gold snake bracelet. She'd seen it before…in Jacinta's shop…on the customer who'd left without giving her a second look!

*"I should have done this myself in the first place,"* Bianca said. *"I assumed his attachment to the woman would keep him from responding to me, but he's been away from her long enough now to have needs."*

Startled by a soft expletive from close behind her, Luz turned to see a furious Quin, his gaze narrowed and focused on the monitor.

Luz stopped the playback. "She's talking about Diego. As prey for some bored rich hunter."

"I'm aware of that."

His tone was cold and yet filled with fury, and for a moment she forgot about the recording.

"How long were you standing there without saying anything?" she asked.

"Long enough to get you killed if I had been Bobby Ray or Carl."

"Bobby Ray isn't in charge," Luz argued. "Bianca is."

Nevertheless, she didn't argue when Quin insisted on leaving any further discoveries until late that night.

She couldn't leave her own discovery though, not without telling him. "Bianca must have been part of the human trafficking operation all along."

"You don't know that."

"Not for sure. But I have instincts, too. They're not reserved for the McKennas."

"And your instincts tell you that her betraying me was what?"

"Planned," Luz returned. "I've seen her before, Quin. In Nuevo Laredo. She was in Jacinta's shop when I walked in to ask about my brother. That was about a half hour before I was taken."

"You're saying Bianca Ramos was responsible for what happened to you?"

"Wouldn't it make sense? They already had Diego. They

came to look through his things, but I beat them to it, so they took me and then went in for their own look."

"Why bring you to a brothel? Why not use you to make him talk?"

"They didn't know who I was. My last name is Delgado, not Ortiz, as they very well knew because they had my purse with all my identification. They probably thought I was a friend of Diego and were going to keep me out of commission until they had what they wanted. Or until they needed to use me."

Quin cursed again. "No wonder I've been dreaming about her—my gift has been trying to warn me that she was more duplicitous than I could even imagine."

Quin packed away the equipment, his expression dark, his stance rigid.

Was he really so angry with *her*? Luz wondered. Or did Bianca still have the power to affect him? It seemed so, especially as he'd been dreaming of her.

"Bobby Ray was looking for you," Quin said stiffly. "I told him you probably had to clean up after disinfecting that stall. He said to get your butt back to the barn ASAP."

"What about you?" She felt as if she'd swallowed a block of ice. "I take it you didn't find Diego."

He shook his head. "I rode the entire northeast quadrant of the property, right up to the fence line. Nothing. Sorry. If I can talk myself onto another horse, I'll see if I can cover more ground."

The way he was speaking to her—so distant and annoyed-sounding—put off Luz. He was thinking of Bianca. Must be. She wanted to believe his reaction was simply that of a man who hated the person who'd done him harm, but she couldn't quite convince herself.

Quin had talked about the McKenna legacy, had admitted he'd thought Bianca was *the one*, but that now he hated her. More likely he hated the fact that he still wanted the woman. Also likely that he wouldn't try to fulfill his grandmother's legacy again.

Which meant she needed to keep a rein on her own emotions, Luz thought.

Between her dislike and fear of his job-related violence and his own unresolved feelings for another woman, Luz knew that caring for Quin was insane.

She should be glad she got to know more about him before things went any farther between them.

She shouldn't be left with a sick feeling in her stomach and an ache in the region of her heart.

TOSSING AND TURNING, Luz came out of a light sleep and stared into the darkened room. For a moment she had to figure out where she was.

Then she remembered.

Although Quin had gotten another ride after lunch, had scoured nearly half the ranch, he hadn't found Diego. And tomorrow, Diego would become the prey for some rich bastard with no morals, no humanity. But first, tonight, Bianca would try to pry the secret of the recording from her brother. Luz only hoped he could resist her better than Quin had.

Quin...

She listened hard but didn't hear him breathing. Eyes adjusting to the dark, she rolled to the other side of the bed and peered down to see an empty sleeping bag on the floor.

"Quin?" she called, her voice sharp, for she was certain he wouldn't answer. "Damn!"

Wondering where he'd gone—whether he'd ridden out in the dark to finish his exploration of ranch land or whether he'd gone back to the house—she made a quick trip to the bathroom, where she flushed her sleep-filled face with water.

Once she felt fully awake, she donned clothes that didn't smell like horse manure and disinfectant.

Even though the moon was nearly full, she doubted Quin would ride out at night. Betting he would wait until just before dawn to go looking for Diego, Luz headed for the house, following the same route they'd taken the night before. Quin had said something about wanting to see what on the computer had so interested Bianca.

She didn't want to think he might go looking for the other woman…

For a moment she imagined that meeting and realized the idea bothered her. More so, the idea of what Quin would do if he found the woman who'd betrayed him. She imagined his hands around Bianca's neck, slowly squeezing the life from her.

He wouldn't do that, Luz assured herself. He was first and foremost a lawman. He would do the right thing.

But what was that?

Immersed in her thoughts, Luz didn't realize she wasn't alone until she was approaching the house. A scuffle came from behind her.

Her pulse thundering, she broke into a run.

# Chapter Fifteen

Breaking into the computer documents had been a no-brainer, but thankfully, Quin had considered *El Jefe* was arrogant enough to use that title as the password. Now he had access to the operation's records—financial transactions for those who'd been trafficked complete with names, addresses and phone numbers of the co-conspirators.

He was sending the last of the files both to his own official ICE e-mail account and to Aaron, with instructions to start closing in on *El Jefe's* partners in crime. He'd already informed Aaron that Diego Ortiz was the intended prize for tomorrow's hunt and asked for backup. In addition, he'd alerted his partner that Pilar had escaped whatever brothel she'd been placed in and asked him to send out a search team for the young woman.

Aaron hadn't responded yet, which probably meant like any sane man, he was asleep in the middle of the night. When Quin was through here, he would call his partner to make sure Aaron would get all the wheels in motion.

Whatever happened, tomorrow would see the end of *El Jefe's* operation, and if Quin's fondest wish was granted, it would be the end of *El Jefe* as well.

When the last file went through, Quin returned the computer

to the way he'd found it. No sense in leaving evidence that he'd been there.

Patting the Dobermans, who'd been standing guard for him, he left the house and headed for the cabin. He would make that call to Aaron, check on Luz, then take out one of the horses before anyone else was up and around. When dawn came, he would be away from the barn and in the area he hadn't yet searched. He was determined to find Luz's brother and free him if it was the last thing he did. He owed that to her and he wanted to give her whatever would make her happy.

Outside the cabin, he placed the call, but got Aaron's voice mail.

"Get up, man, this is it. I e-mailed you evidence and details about *El Jefe's* brothels and work camps. Get on it. And get me backup as soon as you can."

Frustrated that he hadn't actually spoken to his partner, Quin thought about calling his SAC, then decided to give Aaron some time to get back to him. Better that Aaron handle it—he would act first and ask questions later. Not the way SAC Maria Gonzales would. Being that he hadn't let her in on his plan, she would demand an immediate update. Answering questions right now could get him killed if anyone overheard. Besides, he could always call in once he was away from the buildings and searching for Diego.

Silent as a ghost, he entered the cabin the same way he'd left it. He just wanted to check on Luz before taking off to find her brother. Immediately he realized the bed was empty.

His heart slammed against his ribs and he looked around wildly. The bathroom door was open but no one was in there. And nothing in the room seemed to be disturbed. She must have left of her own volition. To find him?

He hadn't seen her on the way to the house, so where the hell was she?

Could she possibly have decided to go off on her own and look for Diego?

*The barn...*

He raced toward it, his thoughts tripping one over the other as he realized the danger in which she'd put herself. The danger for which *he* was responsible. If anything happened to Luz, he wouldn't be able to live with himself.

Legacy or not, Luz Delgado was the one, he realized, fighting panic that threatened to choke him. Luz was the woman he wanted by his side. He wouldn't rest until she was safe in his arms.

By the time he reached the barn, he was wild with fear for her. If she'd ridden out on her own and managed to find her brother, what then? Once inside, he checked every stall and realized none of the horses were missing. Could she have taken one from the pasture?

And if she hadn't, then where the hell was she?

"Looking for something, Quique?" came a familiar voice from behind him. "Or should I say Quin?"

Keeping tight control, Quin turned to face the woman who'd caused him so much misery. Bianca Ramos stood there in the doorway, looking even more beautiful than he remembered. And more deadly. He now recognized the nature of the smile curving her mouth for what it was—poison.

"Bianca, you're looking good," he said, moving slowly toward her. He struggled to stop himself from running to her, wrapping his hands around her throat and squeezing the life from her. "Not at all like a woman trafficked into a bordello."

She laughed. "And you don't look like a man who was trafficked into a work camp. Well, except for the scar." She looked at him slant-eyed while stroking her own cheek. "It adds an interesting aspect to your looks."

"The real scars are inside where you can't see them."

He stopped several feet short of her and scanned her body for potential weapons. She was wearing leather pants and a tank top and he doubted there was any room to hide anything. Therefore, she must have backup nearby.

He tried to get a read on her, but she'd closed herself off from him.

"I've been dreaming about you," he said.

"Sex dreams?"

"Not exactly. Although they have been disturbing in a different way. They kept telling me you weren't who you said you were, that I needed to look beneath the surface." He stared at her, tried to read her but got nothing. She really was expert at hiding her emotions. "At first I thought the dreams were simply reiterating what a betraying bitch you were. Then I realized the message was far more complex."

"And what was the message?"

"I thought you had somehow become *El Jefe's* woman…" His gut clenched at her laugh. "…and then I realized you are *El Jefe.*"

She clapped. "Very good."

Her elation spilled over him. His nailing her identity simply amused her. "And you knew who I was from the first?"

"Of course. I pretended to be a victim to get information on the ICE operation that threatened my empire."

Considering his empathic abilities, Quin couldn't figure out how she'd fooled him so thoroughly. Even now, he couldn't read the stink of evil on her. Perhaps she was using some kind of Aztec magic on him.

"You were good," he admitted. "You fooled me completely."

"I've always had the ability to make people believe I was what they wanted to see. When I was done with you, I should have killed you. Although now I will make a small fortune off you and your supposed brother Luc."

She clapped sharply twice and Bobby Ray came in with Luz in front of him, one arm in a death grip around her neck, the other hand holding a gun to her head.

The breath whooshed out of Quin and it took great effort for him to speak. "It's me you want." He forced himself to speak without emotion. "Let him go."

*"Him?"* Bianca sounded amused. "Please. A short haircut and men's clothing aren't enough to convince me Diego Ortiz's sister is a man."

Quin's gut churned. "How could you know?"

"You were very open in your search for her brother and his woman in Nuevo Laredo. Did you really think no one would come to me with that news? I reward my informants well."

"What have you done with Diego?" Luz cried.

Bianca glanced back at her. "Oh, don't worry, you'll see him before you die. He'll try to save your life by giving me what I want."

"Die?" Luz gasped.

"You'll have a chance to escape, of course, although none of our prey ever does."

A cold that he couldn't shake settled in Quin's middle as Luz cried, "You're going to let someone *hunt* us?"

Bianca laughed again. "Diego will think he can save you and I'll get what *I* want. Our guest will pay double to hunt two of you. Very profitable for *me*. And in the end, *I'll* be rid of the only witnesses. It's a win-win-win situation for me."

"Too late, Bianca," Quin said. "I've sent the information on. Backup is on its way."

She simply laughed yet again and spoke to Bobby Ray. "If he fights you, kill the woman. Now take them to their cage."

Carl came up from behind Quin and grabbed his arm and stuck a gun in his ribs. Bobby Ray was grinning and pressing his gun hard to Luz's head. Quin didn't dare fight them as they forced him forward, past the woman he should have killed rather than tried to save.

"Get some sleep now," Bianca called after them. "You'll need all the energy you can get for the hunt."

LUZ COULDN'T BELIEVE things would end for them this way. Stuck in a dark room with only a bit of moonlight coming in through the caged windows and door, she watched Quin try to figure a way out. But nothing worked—he had no tools to pry loose the lock. The bars were solid.

"Maybe she was right and we should try to get some sleep. You're simply wasting energy."

"How did she know? How?"

"She said she had an informant."

"But who?"

"The only people who knew anything about us or what we were doing were all part of *La Liberación Humana*—Jacinta Herrera, Cesar Galindo, Alma Marquez."

"We don't know about Alma Marquez," Quin said, continuing to test the bars of their prison. "She was supposedly a friend of Pilar but no one ever said she was part of the vigilante group."

"Why would she have given us the crucial information, then? And if she did betray us, why didn't Bianca know the recording was a voice mail?"

"I don't know!" Quin banged his hand against the bars and then shook it as if trying to stem the pain. "There's no way out of here!"

"We'll find a way," she said. "In the morning, when they take us out of here, we'll find a way to escape."

Quin said, "You realize getting away won't be easy. If we manage it, we'll have blood on our hands."

"I thought backup was coming."

"That doesn't mean these men are just going to give up. They're masters of violence."

"Kill or be killed?"

"If it comes to that."

No doubt he believed that this would be the end for them. Luz couldn't face thinking about the threat of violence that would take their lives. She couldn't in her wildest imagination accept that one human being would pay to hunt and kill another human.

Quin sat next to her on the lone narrow bed and wrapped her in his arms. He kissed the top of her head.

"This is my fault," he said softly. "I'm sorry. I never should have let you come."

"You couldn't have stopped me."

"If I'd been in my right mind I could've. I could have had you held for questioning so you couldn't go anywhere. I could have informed your family of your intentions. I imagine your father would have found some way of detaining you."

Luz took a deep breath. Yes, Pappa would have kept her in San Antonio—he would have hired someone to make sure of it.

"It's my fault," she said. "You would have gotten away if Bobby Ray didn't have that gun on me. Or maybe you wouldn't have been caught at all."

"She was warned, remember."

Luz had been thinking about it. Although it seemed Jacinta was the logical traitor—she'd had access to Diego's apartment, had known when he came and went, had known when Luz was there—she had a difficult time believing the older woman was responsible. Her grief had seemed so real. Nor did she believe Alma was responsible.

Could it be Cesar Galindo, then? Could the supposed leader of *La Liberación Humana* be a plant? Or perhaps he had cooperated to get his brother back. Galindo could have sent them to Alma, figuring she might give them information Bianca needed. But what then? Not that thinking about it would help their current situation.

She said, "Do you think they'll offer us a last meal?"

"What?"

"I'm just wondering about the end—"

"Don't think about it that way."

Quin tightened his hold on her and Luz wrapped her arms around his waist and rested her head against his chest. His heartbeat was rapid. Out of fear? Or because he was holding her so close?

If they didn't make it, no one would ever hold her close again.

She would die a virgin—perhaps not literally, but without ever having experienced the joy of a union with a man. Life wasn't fair. Neither was death. But this she could do something about.

Raising her head, she brushed her lips against Quin's.

"What are you doing?" he asked.

"Trying not to think about dying."

She kissed him again.

This time Quin kissed her back. An achingly sweet kiss. Not what Luz needed right now. She wanted something mind-shattering, something that would allow her to push away the fear. She wanted to experience a night in Quin's arms. She wanted to pretend, even if for only one night, that he loved her as much as she loved him.

Pulling out of his arms, Luz climbed on top of Quin, undid his hair from the leather tie and grabbed on to its length with both hands.

"Before I die, I want to know what life is all about." She didn't care if he didn't love her. For one night, she could make it real for herself. "If this is our last night together, then let's make each other happy."

Quin groaned when she kissed him. She slipped her tongue into his mouth, all it took to make him explode with need. He tossed her off him onto her back on the thin mattress and lay over her.

As he kissed her, he moved himself against her so even through their clothes, she could feel him hard between her thighs. She spread her legs and he rocked into her. At the same time, he stroked her breasts through the layers of cloth.

Luz felt as if all her tender places were on fire. She soon burned out of control and pressed into him harder and harder, wanting that elusive something...

"Rock your hips," Quin urged.

She did, lifting her hips higher and higher until her world seemed to pinwheel with bright lights behind her eyes. Her body shuddered and she cried out, but Quin caught the cry with his mouth and smothered it until she was making small sounds of pleasure.

He fumbled between them, loosening their jeans, pulling hers down to her thighs. He tested her with a finger—she was so wet he slipped it inside. The tightness in her middle returned and she tried to ride his hand.

"Not so fast," he whispered, adjusting himself, trading his finger for a thicker instrument of pleasure.

Now he rode her, finger lingering and stroking her clit, putting her in an almost-frenzy, then stopping before she could climax.

"Please," she whispered.

"What?"

"Again," she urged, lifting her hips. "Make it happen again."

He stroked her inside and out and the pressure built and built and this time he didn't stop, not even when she started to come. Not even when she cried out. This time the mind-altering sensations lasted so long, she thought surely she had already died and had gone straight to heaven before he joined her.

It was only later, when she lay in Quin's arms trying to get some sleep, when the roar of a big cat rumbled through her consciousness, that Luz realized that soon enough they would be facing hell together.

## Chapter Sixteen

Their hands were tied behind their backs and nooses were placed around their necks before they were pushed out of the cage by Bobby Ray and Carl.

Bianca Ramos was waiting outside for them. "Do as I say and you'll keep breathing a while longer," the woman who was *El Jefe* said.

Luz was shaking inside, but she refused to show fear, refused to let Bianca see any weakness in her. Quin had convinced her that staying neutral would give them their best chance at survival. Giving way to fear would make them defenseless in the end.

Would make *her* defenseless, Luz thought.

Quin appeared as stoic as ever and she knew he would never be without a plan of action. It wasn't in his nature. He would do whatever it took to survive.

She couldn't say the same for herself.

"So where's Ward?" Quin asked. "Isn't he going to be here for the show?"

Bianca led the way around the corner of the building and Bobby Ray and Carl made sure Luz and Quin followed.

"Ward is just playacting at being the boss," she said. "He's my cover and my lawyer, nothing more. He can't stand the sight of blood. And he doesn't appreciate violence the way some of us do."

Luz knew Bianca included Quin in her assessment.

Kill or be killed…a natural instinct…but could *she* do it if put to the test? Luz wondered.

Was violence ever an acceptable answer to anything?

"Why do you do this?" Luz asked. "Betray your own people?"

"People? Who would they be? I have no family—the ones who didn't starve to death had no health care. My loyalty is reserved for myself."

"Then I feel sorry for you."

Fury crossed Bianca's face only for a second. Then, her expression neutral, she tugged at Quin's noose. "Be a good dog or I'll have Carl break the woman's neck first." She stopped a yard away from what looked to be another holding cell and in a wheedling tone, said, "Diego, you have company."

Luz suddenly came alive. "Diego?" She tried to rush forward to the caged door, but the noose around her neck tightened and jerked her to a stop.

"Not so fast," Carl said.

She could see Diego as he pressed himself against the bars. He was unshaven and thinner than she remembered, but he seemed to be unharmed.

"Luz! What the hell! Are you all right? They didn't hurt you?"

"I'm all right. So is Pilar. She escaped."

"Enough!" Bianca spat.

"What are you doing with my sister?" Diego demanded. "Why have you brought her here?"

"She brought herself, Diego. She thought she was going to rescue you."

Diego threw himself against the bars as if he wanted to get to Bianca…and Bianca simply appeared bored.

"Your sister and her friend here are going to offer us a morning's entertainment."

Diego's tone was wary. "What kind of entertainment?"

"A new client. A hunter."

"No!"

"You can stop it, Diego. Tell me where to find the recording."

"I can tell you that," Quin said. "The recording is on Pilar's cell phone. You already have it."

"Bastard!" Diego yelled.

Quin ignored him. "It's too late anyway, Bianca. I have a copy. Well, my partner at ICE has it along with the evidence I found on your computer."

Luz knew he was lying about the first half. There was nothing on that recording on which he could make an arrest. The recording had stopped too soon, so he hadn't even told Aaron about it.

Quin continued. "My partner's bringing a team in to arrest you all—they'll be here any minute now."

Bianca's visage darkened. "I don't believe any of this. How could you have found the recording if we have the cell?"

"How do you think we found you?" he asked. "Voice mail."

Bianca screeched and went for Quin, hand out to claw his face. Using a foot, he caught her at the back of the knee and she screeched again and went down. Bobby Ray, still holding the noose around his neck, tightened it. Quin resisted and the noose tightened even more.

"Stop it!" Luz yelled. "You'll kill him!"

Bianca got to her feet and dusted herself off. "Don't kill him or he'll be worthless. I want that bounty for both of them."

"Didn't you hear what Quin said?" Luz cried. "Backup is on the way. Run while you have the chance!"

"Because there's no longer any need to negotiate, take them straight to the staging area," Bianca said stiffly, her dark eyes blazing. She checked her watch. "The client will meet us in fifteen minutes. Wait ten before you release them. A five-minute head start should be more than enough."

"Don't do this," Diego begged. "My sister hasn't done anything to you. Let her go. Let them both go."

Bianca simply turned her back on him and walked away.

Carl was pushing at Luz. She tried to get a last look at her brother, but the noose simply tightened so that she saw stars instead.

BOBBY RAY AND CARL rode into the middle of nowhere. Luz felt like she was being strangled if she didn't run fast enough to keep up. She fell once and was dragged by the neck until Quin shouted that Bianca wouldn't appreciate her prey being killed off by anyone other than the hunter. The men slowed the horses some and Luz somehow got back up to her feet and took a ragged breath. Her neck was on fire from rope burn. Her shoulder felt scraped raw, her jeans were torn and she vaguely felt a burn on one leg. She didn't have time to think about it because the men kept their horses moving.

They soon reached a pavilion of sorts in a cleared area in the midst of brush. There was shade, a bench and a horse trough supplied with water by a well with a hand pump.

The men dismounted.

"You have ten minutes before we let you run," Bobby Ray said, leading his horse to the trough. "Better water up."

"Without hands?" Luz asked. "The least you could do is free them."

The foreman snorted. "Yeah, sure. Just stick your face in the water and drink. There's no water between here and the Rio Grande."

"Kind of you to be so concerned," Quin said, squatting and ducking his head down next to one of the horses who was already drinking.

Both men sat on the bench, and while they kept handguns at the ready, they proceeded to take a cigarette break and to talk in low tones.

Knowing she needed water after the run in the heat, Luz took in as much as she could. She was hot as blazes—the sports bra and T-shirt and cotton long-sleeved shirt were all sticking to her wet body—and she wanted in the worst way to throw herself into the trough. But with her hands secured behind her back, how would she ever get out?

"How you doing?" Quin asked softly.

"Surviving." She aimed a poisonous look at their handlers. "And I intend to stay that way."

"Good. Drink more, as much as you can."

Quin gave her a significant look and then turned his gaze to the horse next to him.

What was he up to? Did he think he could get on the horse with no hands? Maybe *he* could, but Luz didn't have his power or his height to help her.

But Quin wasn't making a move away from the trough. He was using the horse as cover, rubbing the rope around his neck on the edge, loosening the noose. He flashed his gaze to Luz as if to make sure she saw what he was doing. She nodded and in between sips of water, did the same, all the while making sure Bobby Ray or Carl didn't catch her. The noose hold gave and for the first time since it was put around her neck, she felt as if she could breathe normally.

"I think that's good," she said, purposely keeping her meaning vague.

Thankfully, she remained still—Bobby Ray gave them a quick look, then turned his attention back to Carl.

Quin was now eyeballing the second horse, who snorted and bobbed his heavy head.

*Ready?* he then mouthed to Luz.

She gave him a sharp nod.

*Now!*

They simultaneously ducked their heads. The noose was up over her nose before anyone noticed.

"Hey, what the hell are you doing?" Bobby Ray shouted.

She ducked her head and pulled it free as did Quin. The men got up from the benches, but Quin whistled twice and yelled and the horses squealed and wheeled.

"What the hell!"

The horses got between them and the armed men. Luz and Quin flew to their feet and ran, Luz throwing a look over her shoulder to see the horses refusing to let Bianca's minions mount them.

"How long will they keep that up?" she asked as she ran.

"Hopefully long enough to give us a good enough head start that I can get our hands free. The longer we have before Bianca and her client come after us, the better."

The area was rife with big mesquites, oak trees, persimmon and black brush. The land to their right inclined upward.

"This way." Quin started climbing.

Was he crazy? She could barely breathe and he wanted her to go up? Then she saw his goal—a fallen tree and some brush that would provide some cover. They slid down out of sight barely a moment before hooves clacked toward them. The horses kept going right past.

"What now?"

"We need to free ourselves." Quin moved away from her and stuck out a leg. "My knife is in my boot." He moved the foot behind her and up against her hands.

Luz felt her way up the boot and then to the inside.

"The other way," Quin instructed.

She adjusted. "Got it." And fumbled with the handle.

"Just hang on to it and I'll move my foot away from your hands."

A tactic that worked. As he slid his foot away, the knife slid out of its sheath.

"Now turn around so we're back-to-back." When they were in position, he said, "Hold it point up for me."

Luz did as he ordered and felt Quin move against her and only prayed he wouldn't cut an artery or he would bleed to death out here.

A few seconds of feeling him move against the blade, he said, "Got it!"

He turned again and took the knife from her and a moment later *her* hands were free.

And then she heard the horses' hooves thunder along the path again. "They're coming back."

Quin wrapped an arm around her and pressed them both tight to the ground. Once more the horses kept going.

"Probably returning to meet Bianca and the hunter."

"Think they'll admit they lost us?"

A moot question. First and foremost, Bobby Ray and Carl would cover their butts. They could say they released the prisoners when ordered and Bianca would have no reason not to believe them.

They took off again, Quin in the lead. Traveling fast but not running, he stayed on rock as much as possible to avoid leaving prints.

"Do you think they'll bring the Dobermans to track us?"

"That might not be a problem," Quin said.

Although Luz wondered whether the dogs would turn against their mistress, they probably had no loyalty to the hands and definitely none to the hunter.

The sun was high and the day was getting hotter. Sheer exhaustion and stress were taking their toll on Luz. She didn't know how much longer she could keep going.

As if he knew what she was thinking, Quin slowed a bit but said, "We need to push on until we reach the river."

"How much farther?" she choked out.

"I don't know, but we're headed in the right direction."

They went through brush and a stand of trees only to find themselves in the open, surrounded by a crown of rock. They were in a canyon of sorts and there was only one direction left for them to take. They kept going until Luz imagined she heard a rush of water nearby. Rapids?

"The river!" she gasped even as the earth trembled beneath her feet.

She ran faster, saw the drop-off. A cliff. Her stomach roiled and she tripped, nearly fell. Glancing back, she saw four horses thunder to a stop. Four horses and two big cats in a cage on wheels. Mountain lions. Bobby Ray dismounted, some kind of cloth in his hand. He opened the cage and threw the cloth inside.

One of the big cats roared and rolled, mock fighting what looked like one of their bathroom towels.

"What the hell?" she gasped as Quin grabbed her by the arm and hauled her to her feet.

Still, she didn't move. What was the point when the hunting party was within shouting distance, the humans were armed and both cats had their scent and were now coming straight for them and a death-defying drop lay behind?

QUIN knew it was too late to run.

They couldn't outrun the cats. Not that there was anywhere to run except into the river—the fall itself would probably kill them.

He concentrated on the mountain lions, gave them a series of low whistles to get their attention, to keep them away from

Luz. Her pheromones would reveal her fear and they would go straight for her if he didn't interfere now.

Both cats turned their attention to him. They began stalking him. Quin stared one straight in the eyes, then the other, swiftly making the connection that was always thankfully there for him with animals. They hesitated, seeming confused by the signals he was giving them.

He concentrated, drew images in his mind, visualized Bianca and the hunter, who had shouldered his rifle from its sheath and now was adjusting the scope. No time. He quickly transmitted more visuals, showing the cats what he wanted them to do.

One mountain lion turned back immediately, bounding up a tree that took it above the hunting party.

The second cat wasn't as easily swayed. He eyed Luz for his next meal. As the hunter raised his rifle, Quin gave a sharp whistle and projected a more insistent image, and with a roar, the mountain lion swung back and followed his partner, already leaping from a tree limb onto the man.

Quin watched as the scene played itself out slowly.

The big cat ripped into the hunter, who screamed and triggered the rifle. Shots went wild and the cat bounded off and the man's blood sprayed everywhere as he toppled from his horse like a dropped sack of potatoes.

Bianca was screaming, too, at Bobby Ray and Carl, who were riding away in a cloud of dust. The woman turned her mount to follow when the second cat leaped, its jaws meeting the side of her head before throwing her off her horse and then bounding off to join up with his companion.

The threat over, Quin looked to Luz, who stood wide-eyed and still as death, as if the violence against the villains horrified her more than the thought of death itself.

He couldn't let her stop him from finishing his job. Besides, there was Diego to consider. Who the hell knew what Bobby Ray or Carl would do?

He took her by the arm and started moving toward the horses. "Let's go get your brother."

Although she let him lead her, she nodded toward Bianca and the hunter, both of whom lay on the ground. "What about them?"

The man's body was going into spasms. Bianca covered her face and wailed. The big cats were perched on some nearby boulders, cleaning themselves.

"I'll send backup to get them."

"You mean their bodies," Luz said, her voice faint.

"They're both still alive. I wanted the cats to put them out of commission, not kill them."

He whistled and forced an image of the area they'd ridden through in the cats' minds. Reluctantly, it seemed, the mountain lions rose and sauntered off.

Luz still seemed shaky, so he helped her onto Bianca's horse and he mounted the hunter's.

"You'll die for this, both of you!" Bianca screeched.

Quin looked back at her ruined beauty. One side of her face was torn, the flesh hanging in shreds. Not punishment enough for the things she had been responsible for over the past several years.

But it was a start.

Quin urged his mount forward. Luz's followed close behind. He wanted in the worst way to talk to her, to tell her how he felt about her, to hold her and thank God she was still alive…but she remained silent and stiff in the saddle and the truth was she looked more fragile than he'd ever seen her.

His own needs could wait.

What Luz needed now was her brother. Seeing Diego alive and well would reassure her that everything they'd gone through—everything he'd done—had been necessary to rescue her brother and themselves. God knew what Bobby Ray and Carl would do to him because he'd seen their faces.

He urged the horses faster, gave his horse its head and soon they were flying for home. They arrived at the outbuildings where Diego was being held not a moment too soon.

Gun in hand, Carl was at Diego's caged door.

"Stop right there, Carl!" Quin yelled before the man could shoot.

Carl whipped around, took a shot but missed.

"Luz, get away!" Quin yelled.

His only weapon being the knife, he simultaneously ducked and reached into his boot, and as another shot rang out, grabbed and flipped the knife straight into Carl's throat.

Gagging, Carl pulled it out along with a rush of blood. Meaning to stop the flow so the bastard wouldn't die on him—he needed live witnesses—Quin dismounted.

Just then, Bobby Ray came around the far side of the building. "Is the Mexican dead yet or what?"

"Or what!" Quin answered.

A burst of adrenaline driving him, Quin launched himself at the foreman and took him down. They rolled in the dust and traded punches. Bobby Ray pressed his thumbs into Quin's eyes, but Quin plunged his hands between the other man's arms and chopped outward. Once free and able to see again, he aimed for the man's gut, but Bobby Ray rolled and as Quin came after him, kicked out hard. He got Quin good, boot-to-jaw, and left him stunned long enough that Bobby Ray was able to get to his feet and draw his gun.

"I knew you were going to be trouble, Quique or whatever your name is. Luckily, we know how to handle trouble in this part of the country."

He aimed straight at Quin's head—no one could miss at this short distance.

A shot rang out, but Quin felt no pain.

Blood burbled out of Bobby Ray's mouth. The foreman went limp…dropped to his knees…then landed face down on the dirt inches away from Quin.

Standing there in front of him, wild-eyed and white as a ghost, Luz still had a two-handed grip on the handgun she must've gotten off of Carl.

Even as Quin got to his feet, meaning to reassure her, searching for the words that would make what she'd been forced to do all right for her, Quin heard the chopper and glanced back over his shoulder.

"Luz, are you all right?" Diego called as backup arrived— a helicopter above and a string of official vehicles, lights blipping, on the road below. "Luz!"

She was still standing shock-still.

Turning over Bobby Ray's body, Quin unclipped a keyring and within seconds found the one that opened Diego's cell door.

Then he stood back and watched the woman he loved throw her arms around her brother's neck and weep as if she would never stop.

# Chapter Seventeen

"Hey, how you doing, Luz?" Diego asked, coming up behind her as she poured a mug of coffee.

She'd been counting the hours and minutes since they'd been rescued. They'd been held at ICE for more than twenty-four hours, but had been allowed to come back to her apartment yesterday.

"I'm fine." Luz forced out a smile to reassure her brother. "You did what you had to do."

Luz stiffened. "You mean kill someone?"

"I mean you protected someone you cared about. I would have done anything to protect Pilar."

Thankfully, Pilar was safe now. She and Diego had stayed with Luz the night before. Luz had gladly given them her bedroom. She hadn't done more than doze on the couch, anyway, with Blossom perched on the arm over her head. Every time she'd started to fall asleep, she'd felt the gun in her hands as it had gone off…and in the middle of the night, she'd found herself walking around the courtyard.

"I protected my world for five years…since Gus…I never thought I would ever have to resort to using violence myself…"

"Sometimes we don't have a choice," Diego said, wrapping his arms around her and kissing the top of her head. "We do what we have to for survival."

Knowing now that Diego and Pilar had been working with *La Liberación Humana* to free their countrymen, she asked, "Have you ever had to kill anyone?"

Diego's gaze slid away from her. "I think I hear Pilar moving around. Let me see how long she'll be."

A sick feeling welled up in her as Diego avoided answering her question. "I need to feed the cat before leaving again."

As she opened the can of tuna, Blossom wound her plush body around Luz's legs. The contact lightened Luz's heart, but only for a moment.

She couldn't help but wonder how well her brother slept at night. And wondered what Pilar had done to escape the brothel—had she been forced to kill someone, too?

Thankfully, after escaping, Pilar had turned herself into the local authorities, who had informed ICE of her whereabouts. All four of them had been checked out by doctors and therapists, then had been thoroughly debriefed by Special Agents. Luz had barely seen Quin during that time, however, and when she had, she'd had a difficult time meeting his gaze.

She set the dish of food by the cat's water bowl. "There you go, sweetheart."

Blossom looked at her and Luz patted the cat's back, stroked her length from spine to tail. Happy now, Blossom started to eat.

If only happiness for humans could be so simple.

She had a lot to process, difficult with so much happening, including an unexpected visit from her parents who'd wanted to reassure themselves that she was all right after she'd called from the ICE offices.

Pappa had even tried to make a connection with his son for once, but Diego had kept Pappa at bay. No doubt her brother didn't trust that Pappa's feelings wouldn't regress once time passed. She didn't blame him. Pappa had been such a jackass where Diego was concerned and now he wanted to know every detail of what had happened to his children, wanted to know how long it would be before the trial began.

Mamma had simply been glad to hold her daughter again and had been equally warm and welcoming with Diego and Pilar.

The trial…Luz had no idea of when that would be. The wheels of the justice system turned slowly.

Her and Diego's sworn statements added to Quin's would make the case against Bianca Ramos. Luz wondered how much of her life the head of the crime syndicate would spend behind bars or if it would quickly end on death row.

Bobby Ray was dead, although Carl and Bianca's client were still alive. Luz supposed they would have separate trials. She didn't look forward to being in those courtrooms, but she would testify to see that justice was done.

"Luz, ready to go?" Diego called from the bedroom.

"Coming."

They were planning on going out for breakfast in the car Diego had rented—one of the agents at ICE had helped replace his documents and credit cards. They were planning on trying to act like life had gone back to normal.

Luz didn't know what normal was supposed to be anymore.

Her world had been turned upside down. Everything she'd believed in seemed different. Trite. After Gus's death, she used to ask herself whether violence was ever necessary.

Now she knew that sometimes it was.

Killing a man had changed her—everything she'd gone through in the last week had changed her—and she couldn't ever go back to being that naive young woman she'd once been. Even after having been trafficked, humiliated, nearly shot, she'd still thought that she could never be with a man like Quin because of his profession, because of the violence that was part of his life. But now she realized it was part of hers as well.

Her worldview had changed dramatically. She saw that Quin wanted to help people who couldn't help themselves with a passion she could only envy. A passion she wished for herself…and hadn't even known it until now.

Now Luz regretted having lived half a life for far too long, and it seemed to her that Quinlan McKenna Farrell was just what she needed to be fully alive again.

*If he felt the same way about her…*

Considering she hadn't heard from Quin personally by now, Luz feared she never would.

She'd fallen in love fully and completely for the first time in her life and now before that love even had a chance to bloom, she feared it was over.

"HEY, IT'S OVER. Can you believe it?" Aaron asked Quin.

"It's not really over—not yet."

They were alone in the break room. Nursing a mug of coffee, Quin wished he was with Luz instead of here…not that she would want him. Not after she'd shot Bobby Ray because of him.

"C'mon, Quin, you single-handedly brought down *El Jefe's* operation. We've already closed five brothels and three work camps with illegals and more women plying the trade out of trailers. We've filled several jail cells with criminals and are taking care of dozens of people who were virtual prisoners. You have to feel good about that."

"I'll feel good when all the loose ends are tied up."

"Well, right," Aaron said, leaning back in his chair. "The trial. Who knows when that'll be? In the meantime, take credit where credit is due."

Quin took a last slug of coffee to bolster him and then set down the mug. "Bianca said she had an informant."

Aaron started. "What? Well, yeah, sure, that makes sense. She probably has lots of them."

Aaron still didn't get it.

"Luz and I tried to figure the identity of this informant. The only people we had direct contact with in Nuevo Laredo were Jacinta Herrera, Diego's landlady, Cesar Galindo, head of the vigilantes, Alma Marquez, Pilar's friend, and Mrs. Morales, Pilar's mother. That any of them would have reason to turn on us didn't make sense."

"What makes you think one of them did?"

"I don't. I think it was someone else. Someone who knew what we were up to when we headed for Hunt Ranch. Someone who thought we had access to a recording that could be used as evidence." Sensing Aaron's anxiety level increasing, Quin looked straight at his partner. "I never told you what was on that recording, Aaron. I never told you Pilar transmitted it to her voice mail, but that the information about what was going on at the ranch was incomplete. Nothing we could hang a conviction on."

"Quin, what are you trying to say?"

Aaron's guilt enveloped Quin like shrink-wrap. Quin felt sick inside. He'd been pretty certain it had been Aaron who'd sold him out, but he hadn't wanted to admit it. His partner and his supposed friend had betrayed him for what?

"Why?" he asked. "I don't get it."

Aaron turned pasty white and a film of sweat broke out on his forehead. "I don't know what you're talking about."

"How stupid do you think I am, Aaron?"

Quin waited while Aaron's guilt shifted into panic on overdrive. He stared at the man he had so foolishly trusted with not only his life, but with the life of the woman he loved.

Aaron licked his lips. "It wasn't supposed to be like this, Quin. I needed money bad. You gotta understand Mom didn't just go into a nursing home. She had to go to an Alzheimer's facility. Do you know how much that costs? I would have gone through our savings, through the kids' college fund, before the first year was up. I needed money and suddenly there was a way to get it. All I had to do was share some information about the investigation. I thought that one time would be it and I would be out."

"When?"

"Before...um...before you got trafficked into the work camp."

So Aaron was responsible for that, too.

He continued, talking fast. "I never had any idea that you were going to disappear, Quin. I was so happy when you escaped. I wasn't going to do anything more for them after that, I swear, but then they threatened my kids, said they knew where they went to school and wouldn't it be a shame if they never came home someday. What the hell was I supposed to do?"

Quin didn't know. "Betray me, I guess."

"I saved your damn life! I saved you all! Twice I got backup there in time. In the end, I couldn't do what *El Jefe* wanted, not if it meant you had to die."

Aaron's desperation poured out of him. Quin believed him, but it didn't make a difference. Even though he was grateful for his partner's change of heart, Aaron had taken dirty money to betray the investigation.

And him.

Taking a deep breath, Quin said, "You can come in now."

"Who can come in?" Aaron looked around wildly. "Who are you talking to?"

Quin peeled back the edge of his jacket to show he was wired for sound.

A moment later, two armed men escorted SAC Maria Gonzales into the room.

And a heavy-hearted Quin left it, possibly for the last time.

"WE NEED TO GET HOME," Diego said, his arm around Pilar's waist as they entered Luz's apartment. "Back to Mexico."

Looking up at him with pure love in her dark eyes, Diego's woman appeared so darn young and innocent. Good thing she was resilient.

Every so often over the past two days, Luz had caught a look of fright or anger in Pilar's gaze, but for the most part, Pilar stayed strong. She, too, had spoken to a therapist and promised to continue doing so when she got back to Nuevo Laredo, but Luz guessed Pilar's having a man who stood by her no matter what had happened to her in that brothel was the best medicine.

It would certainly do *her* a world of good to have Quin by her side, Luz thought, feeling empty without him.

A feeling she was going to have to get used to.

She only hoped the therapist she intended to see could help.

"*Mami* and *Papi* won't rest until they see me with their own eyes," Pilar said.

"We're already packed," Diego said of the few items they'd bought—it all fit in one small bag. "Time to get on the road."

"What if it isn't safe to go home yet?" Luz didn't want to lose her brother so soon after finding him again. "We don't know that all the arrests have been made."

"With ICE on the back of the Mexican authorities, I'm not too worried," Diego assured her. "They'll want to end the international embarrassment as quickly as possible."

Pilar added, "And Cesar says he'll have men watching over us until it's done."

"The two of you are so brave."

"Not any braver than my sister," Diego said.

"I was terrified the whole time."

"Fear doesn't negate bravery, Luz. You acted as you were forced to do by conscience and love. No matter how scared you were, you didn't stop until you found me." He put his arms around her and hugged her tight. "I will never forget that. You will always be part of my heart."

And now he was going back to Mexico, putting distance between them again. The backs of her eyes stung, but Luz refused to let tears fall. Diego and Pilar had been through so much, she wouldn't be a burden to them.

"Go, then. Just make sure you call me every day."

He kissed the top of her head and stepped back. "I promise."

"What about this Quin of yours?" Pilar asked.

"He's not my Quin."

"I saw how you looked at him when you thought he didn't see," Pilar said. "And how he looked at you. Are you certain he isn't yours?"

Wishing it were so, Luz said, "Quin didn't try to get me alone at the ICE offices. And he hasn't tried to contact me here. I think he may still be in love with Bianca Ramos."

"I never was in love with her."

Gasping "Quin!" at hearing his voice, Luz whipped around to see him standing in the open doorway. Caught by his intense blue gaze, she couldn't say another word.

"I'll just get our bag." Diego left the room.

"Aren't you going to ask me in?"

It was Pilar who gestured and said, "Please."

Quin entered the apartment as Diego came out of the bedroom, the bag with their things hooked over his shoulder. He hugged and kissed Luz, then held out his hand to Quin, who took it.

"I can't ever thank you enough for what you did."

"You can testify."

"Count on it."

"We both will," Pilar said, standing on tiptoe to hug Quin. "And don't go missing again."

Diego snaked an arm around his woman's waist and turned

her toward the door. "Not if we can help it." He paused and
looked from Luz to Quin. "Take care of my sister." Then they
left the apartment.

Luz was left standing in the middle of the room, not
knowing what to say. Her pulse picked up and she found it
impossible to breathe normally. She'd just been thinking about
Quin—mourning his loss—and he appeared as though her
thoughts had brought him.

"Why are you here?" she finally asked. "You could have
called me."

"I *should* have called you. Not about the case, just to see
how you were." His gaze was all over her, as if he couldn't
get enough. "So how are you?"

"Alive."

"I see."

Luz could tell there was more on his mind. "What else,
Quin? What's happened?"

"I nailed the informant."

"Cesar Galindo?"

He shook his head.

"Not Jacinta—"

"Aaron," he said. "I can thank my partner for the time I
spent in that work camp. And for what happened to us at
Hunt Ranch. He's not an evil man. He didn't want to see
anyone dead. First he was desperate for money to take care
of his mother, then he had to protect his kids. The last was his
fault, really. There is no easy way without consequences."

"Oh, Quin…" Without thinking, Luz crossed to him and
put her hand on his chest and felt his heart beat hard against
her fingers. "I'm so sorry."

When he covered her hand with his, her blood slid through
her in a rush that left her light-headed.

"I'm sorry, too. I never should have taken you with me. I

should have turned you over to Maria, had her hold you for questioning while I ran the investigation."

She pulled her hand away from him as she asked, "You're sorry you got to know me?"

"Of course not. But the things that we went through... Bobby Ray...that never should have happened to you. You never should have had to make that choice."

"If I hadn't been there, you might be dead."

"Better than killing what's inside you."

"I'm not dead inside, Quin. Wounded, maybe. But I still feel. And I'm glad that you're alive." She wouldn't tell him that if he'd been killed, she would have wanted to die, too.

"I thought you hated me."

"I was in shock. Don't get me wrong—I hated what I did— that I had to do it. And I *did* have to. I couldn't let you die, not any more than I could let Diego disappear without doing everything in my power to find him."

"But he's your brother and you love him."

Heat flushed through her and she looked down so he couldn't see her face, couldn't see into her eyes.

"Luz...you care about me?"

"Of course. After everything we went through together."

"I don't mean that. I feel it. A want...a yearning... something deeper...it all shimmers off you."

Remembering Quin was an empath, Luz groaned. "The McKenna legacy. But maybe you're reading a little too much—"

"Am I? Let me tell you something about the legacy and the reason I thought Bianca was the right woman for me. My grandmother wrote: *within thirty-three days of your thirty-third birthday*—"

"And that's when you met her."

"Right. On my birthday. And I met you on the thirty-third day after. I went back and counted."

Startled, she asked, "Why would you do that?"

"I needed an explanation. The legacy could have come true for my siblings and cousins but not for me. Or so I thought. I needed to know how I could have fallen so madly in love with you against my grandmother's prophecy."

She could suddenly feel her heart bang against her ribs. "You love me?"

"I was fated to meet you and act in your behalf because *you* are my legacy. Yes, Luz, I'm crazy in love with you. I can't stop thinking about you. And I know you care about me. But after everything that's happened, is that enough that you would give me a chance? Give us a chance?"

Words Luz had feared she would never hear. She pulled his head down. "I'd like to try," she whispered, then kissed him.

They were so intrinsically different, she didn't know if they stood a chance together, but through with hiding from life, she was going to throw caution to the wind and believe in the McKenna legacy with all her heart.

# Epilogue

Quin had never been so happy as he was when he and Luz went out for a ride on the family ranch.

"It's a beautiful spread," Luz said, dismounting and looking out over hundreds of acres of grazing land and forest. "South Dakota is so different from Texas. So much more lush."

"So you like it?"

"I love it."

Waves of Luz's happiness flowed over him and Quin took a breath of relief. "Would you consider moving here?"

They'd known each other for six weeks, but Quin didn't think he could know Luz any better in six months or in six years. He wouldn't know his mind any better.

"Are you asking because you plan to move back here?"

"I'm asking because I want to make a life with you, Luz. I want us to grow old together. I want a safe place to raise a family. Will you marry me and become a rancher's wife?"

"No! You're a lawman."

"You hate violence."

"I love *you* and want you to be happy. A man's work is who he is. Maybe you can be a lawman here in South Dakota. Work for the county or a town."

He'd already resigned from his job as a federal agent, but that didn't mean he couldn't get another one with far less risk. "You sure about that?"

"I'm sure I want you to be happy," Luz said.

"I would be happy being anywhere, doing anything with you."

"For a while, maybe. I don't want you to regret anything. I want us both to do what'll make us happy and fulfilled. I'm not hiding from life ever again."

He'd seen the change in her. At first he'd feared killing Bobby Ray would ruin any chance they had. But she'd somehow dealt with the act and had been helping Diego and *La Liberación Humana* find the missing. He was certain she would want to get involved with a good cause wherever they were. And he wanted it to be here, with family. His family that he'd virtually abandoned for too many years.

"What about your own family? Diego? Are you sure you'd be okay leaving them?"

"I'm never going to leave them. I just won't see them as often. We can go back to visit, right?"

"Absolutely. And they can come here, too. So, will you marry me?" he asked again.

"Yes." Luz threw herself against him. "Oh, yes!"

Grinning, Quin couldn't wait to tell the family that the McKenna legacy finally had come full circle.

LUZ LOVED QUIN'S parents, Rose and Charlie, and siblings, Kate and Neil, and in-laws, Chase and Annabeth, and niece and nephew, Maggie and Jeremy, and they all seemed to love her, so there was great celebration around the dinner table after Quin made the announcement of their engagement and intended move to South Dakota.

"It's about time!" Neil said, slapping his younger brother on the back.

"Told you so." Kate grinned and leaned into her husband, Chase.

"Oh, my," Rose said, her eyes tearing up, "All my children married and around me at last."

Charlie patted his wife's arm. "A woman who can keep control over our boy." He winked at Luz.

Luz couldn't stop smiling. She'd never been so happy. "I can't believe I'm inheriting this big, wonderful family."

"A family that's about to get bigger," Rose announced.

"Who's pregnant?" Quin asked.

"No one's pregnant," his mother said. She looked from her daughter to daughter-in-law and asked, somewhat hopefully, "Are you?"

"No!" Kate and Annabeth said together.

Sighing, Rose explained, "A relative is coming from Ireland this summer. He's going to stay with us a while. His name is Tiernan McKenna and he's your second cousin," she told her children. "Or is it second cousin once removed? Oh, I'm not sure, but he's family."

"Why does he want to come here?" Charlie asked.

"He's says he's always wanted to cowboy."

Neil laughed. "What makes him think he's qualified to work on a ranch?"

"He works with horses in Ireland."

"Must be Thoroughbreds," Chase said, laughing, too. "Well, he's not all clueless, then."

"We'll give him a chance," Annabeth said.

"Good." Rose beamed. "There's always room for one more in our family."

A statement that warmed Luz's heart. She couldn't wait to be part of them all.

\* \* \* \* \*

*Watch for Tiernan McKenna and the first story about
a new branch of the McKennas. STEALING THUNDER
will be published next August as part of
Harlequin Intrigue's 25th anniversary.*

*Celebrate 60 years of pure reading pleasure with*
*Harlequin®!*

*Step back in time and enjoy a sneak preview of an exciting*
*anthology from Harlequin® Historical with*
*THE DIAMONDS OF WELBOURNE MANOR*

This compelling anthology features three stories about
the outrageous Fitzmanning sisters. Meet Annalise, who
is never at a loss for words... But that can change with
an unexpected encounter in the forest.

*Available May 2009 from Harlequin® Historical.*

"I'm the illegitimate daughter of notoriously scandalous parents, Mr. Milford. Candidates for my hand are unlikely to be lining up at the gates."

"Don't be so quick to discount your charms, my dear. Or the charm of your substantial dowry. Or even your brothers' influence. There are as many reasons to marry as there are marriages."

Annalise snorted. "Oh, yes. Perhaps I shall marry for dynastic reasons, or perhaps for property or influence. After all, a loveless, practical marriage worked out so well for my mother."

"Well, you've routed me on that one. I can think of no suitable rejoinder." Ned rose to his feet and extended his hand. "And since that is the case, let me be the first to wish you a long and happy spinsterhood."

Her mouth gaped open. And then she laughed.

And he froze.

This was the first time, Ned realized. The first time he'd seen her eyes light up and her mouth curl. The first time he'd witnessed her features melded together in glorious accord to produce exquisite beauty.

Unbelievable what a change came over her face. Unheard of what effect her throaty, rasping laughter had on his body.

It pounded a beat upon his ear, quickly taken up by his pulse. It echoed through him, finally residing in his stirring nether regions.

So easily she did it, awakened these sensations within him—without any apparent effort at all. And she had called him potentially dangerous? Clearly the intelligent thing for him to do would be to steer clear, to leave her to the tender ministrations of Lord Peter Blackthorne.

"You were right." She smiled up at him as she took his hand and climbed to her feet. "I do feel better."

Ah, well. When had he ever chosen the intelligent path?

He did not relinquish her hand. He used it to pull her in, close enough that he could feel the warmth of her. "At the risk of repeating Lord Peter's mistake and anticipating too much— may I ask if you'll be my partner in battledore tomorrow?"

Her smiled dimmed. Her breath came a little faster. His own had gone shallow, as if he'd just run a race—and lost. He ran his gaze over the appealing lift of her brow and the curious angle of her chin. His index finger twitched.

"I should like that," she said.

His finger trembled again and he lifted it, traced the pink and tender shell of her ear, the unique sweep of her jaw. Her pulse leaped beneath her skin, triggering his own. Slowly he tilted her chin up, waiting for her to object, to step back, to slap his hand away.

She did none of those eminently sensible things. Which left him free to do the entirely impractical thing.

Baby soft, the skin of her lips. Her whole body trembled when he touched her there.

He leaned in. Her eyes closed, even as she stood straight against him, strung as tight as a bow. He pressed his mouth to hers. It was a soft kiss, sweet and chaste. And yet he was hot and hard and as ready as he'd ever been in his life.

She drew back a little. Sighed. Their breath mingled a moment before she slowly backed away.

"Oh," she breathed. Her dark eyes were full of wonder and something that looked like fear. He took a step toward her, but she only shook her head. His outstretched hand fell to his side as she turned to disappear into the wood. This was the first time, Ned realized. The first time, since he'd come to the house party at Welbourne Manor, that he'd seen her eyes light up.

\* \* \* \* \*

*Follow Ned and Annalise's story in May 2009 in*
*THE DIAMONDS OF WELBOURNE MANOR*
*Available May 2009 from Harlequin® Historical*

*Available in the series romance section, or in the historical*
*romance section, wherever books are sold.*

We'll be spotlighting a different series every month throughout 2009 to celebrate our 60th anniversary.

## Look for Harlequin® American Romance® in June!

Join us for a year-long celebration of the rugged American male! From cops to cowboys— Men Made in America has the hero you've been dreaming about!

Look for

# The Chief Ranger

### by Rebecca Winters, on sale in June!

| | |
|---|---|
| *Bachelor CEO* by Michele Dunaway | July |
| *The Rodeo Rider* by Roxann Delaney | August |
| *Doctor Daddy* by Jacqueline Diamond | September |

# REQUEST YOUR FREE BOOKS!

## 2 FREE NOVELS
## PLUS 2
## FREE GIFTS!

**◆ HARLEQUIN®**

# INTRIGUE®

## Breathtaking Romantic Suspense

**YES!** Please send me 2 FREE Harlequin Intrigue® novels and my 2 FREE gifts (gifts are worth about $10). After receiving them, if I don't wish to receive any more books, I can return the shipping statement marked "cancel." If I don't cancel, I will receive 6 brand-new novels every month and be billed just $4.24 per book in the U.S. or $4.99 per book in Canada. That's a savings of close to 15% off the cover price! It's quite a bargain! Shipping and handling is just 25¢ per book*. I understand that accepting the 2 free books and gifts places me under no obligation to buy anything. I can always return a shipment and cancel at any time. Even if I never buy another book from Harlequin, the two free books and gifts are mine to keep forever.

182 HDN EEZ7   382 HDN EEZK

| | |
|---|---|
| Name | (PLEASE PRINT) |

| | |
|---|---|
| Address | Apt. # |

| | | |
|---|---|---|
| City | State/Prov. | Zip/Postal Code |

Signature (if under 18, a parent or guardian must sign)

### Mail to the Harlequin Reader Service:
**IN U.S.A.:** P.O. Box 1867, Buffalo, NY 14240-1867
**IN CANADA:** P.O. Box 609, Fort Erie, Ontario L2A 5X3

Not valid to current subscribers of Harlequin Intrigue books.

**Are you a current subscriber of Harlequin Intrigue books
and want to receive the larger-print edition?
Call 1-800-873-8635 today!**

* Terms and prices subject to change without notice. Prices do not include applicable taxes. Sales tax applicable in N.Y. Canadian residents will be charged applicable provincial taxes and GST. Offer not valid in Quebec. This offer is limited to one order per household. All orders subject to approval. Credit or debit balances in a customer's account(s) may be offset by any other outstanding balance owed by or to the customer. Please allow 4 to 6 weeks for delivery. Offer available while quantities last.

**Your Privacy:** Harlequin is committed to protecting your privacy. Our Privacy Policy is available online at www.eHarlequin.com or upon request from the Reader Service. From time to time we make our lists of customers available to reputable third parties who may have a product or service of interest to you. If you would prefer we not share your name and address, please check here. ☐

H109

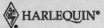